"I could pay the debts for you."

Carton continued, "And give your father the house. I could pay everything off."

"I don't understand," Katie said weakly.

"I think you do. I want you, Katie. I want you very badly."

"You're seriously saying you want to buy me? You want me to be your mistress?"

"No!" The explosion was immediate. "I want to marry you—after which, every debt would be cleared. The grand sacrifice, or a way of escape.... Decision time, little Katie White!"

HELEN BROOKS lives in Northamptonshire, England, and is married with three children. As she is a committed Christian, busy housewife and mother, her spare time is at a premium but her hobbies include reading and walking her two energetic and very endearing young dogs. Her long-cherished aspiration to write became a reality when she put pen to paper on reaching the age of forty, and sent the result off to Harlequin.

Helen Brooks now concentrates on writing for Harlequin Presents®, with highly emotional, poignant yet intense books we know you'll love!

Books by Helen Brooks

Don't miss any of our special offers. Write to us at the following address for information on our newest releases.

Harlequin Reader Service
U.S.: 3010 Walden Ave., P.O. Box 1325, Buffalo, NY 14269
Canadian: P.O. Box 609, Fort Erie, Ont. L2A 5X3

HELEN BROOKS

The Marriage Solution

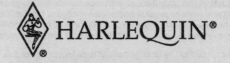

HARLEQUIN®

TORONTO • NEW YORK • LONDON
AMSTERDAM • PARIS • SYDNEY • HAMBURG
STOCKHOLM • ATHENS • TOKYO • MILAN • MADRID
PRAGUE • WARSAW • BUDAPEST • AUCKLAND

ISBN 0-373-11987-9

THE MARRIAGE SOLUTION

First North American Publication 1998.

CHAPTER ONE

'I NEED to speak to David White *now*.'

Katie raised an eyebrow at the phone as she moved it back an inch or two from her ear before answering the hard male voice in a polite but firm tone. 'I'm sorry, I'm afraid my father can't be disturbed at the moment. Can I take—?'

'The hell he can't!' Now the voice was patently insulting with a thread of undeniable steel in its dark depths. 'Put me through, Miss White.'

'I can't do that.' She had straightened, her slim body held tight and still and her voice cool. 'I've told you, he can't be disturbed—'

'He'll be more than disturbed when I've finished with him.' She flinched visibly even as she wondered what on earth her father had done to make someone so mad. 'And I'm not asking, Miss White, I'm *telling* you. Put me through—'

'No.' There was a split second of icy silence before she followed through. 'My father isn't well; the doctor is with him now.'

'The doctor?' She heard him swear under his breath, a particularly explicit oath which would have been quite at place in a rugby club changing-room, before he spoke again in clipped, measured tones that suggested barely controlled rage. 'Then when he has finished with the doctor I expect a call immediately. Is that clear?'

'Now look, Mr...?'

'Reef. Carlton Reef.'

'Well, I'm sorry, Mr Reef,' she said stiffly, 'but I have

5

no intention of bothering my father with mundane business matters today. I presume it *is* business you wish to discuss with him?' she added icily.

'Dead right, Miss White,' he shot back tightly. 'And, for your information, the loss of a great deal of money due to your father's stupidity and crass ineptitude I do not consider mundane. I can be reached in my office for the next hour, after which the matter goes into the hands of my solicitors and I won't be accepting any calls from that point from either your father or his lackeys. Is that clear enough for you or shall I repeat it?'

'Mr Reef—'

'Which daughter are you anyway?' he interrupted her abruptly. 'Katie or Jennifer?'

'Katie.' She took a deep breath as she leant limply against the wall and prayed that the shaking which had begun in her stomach wouldn't transfer itself to her voice. This was incredible, monstrous—there had to be a perfectly simple explanation. 'Mr Reef, I'm sure there's a mistake here somewhere.'

'So am I,' he agreed coldly, 'and your father is the one who made it. I won't be made a fool of, Miss White, and I thought your father had the sense to realise that. One hour—doctor or no doctor.' And the phone went dead.

She remained staring at the receiver in her hand for a good thirty seconds before she recovered sufficiently to replace it and sink down on the nearest seat in the massive wide hall. This would have to happen today, with her father so ill.

The pains that had started in his chest during breakfast as he had read his paper had culminated within minutes in his writhing on the floor in agony, with Katie kneeling at his side as their housekeeper had frantically called the family doctor, who was also Katie's father's close friend, and fortunately lived in the same exclusive avenue of large detached houses. He had arrived within two or three minutes, just as the housekeeper, Mrs Jenkins, had taken the call from this Reef man, who had insisted on speaking to one of the family when Mrs Jenkins had told him that her employer wasn't available.

She had to get back to her father. She took a long, shuddering breath and levered herself off the seat before she hurried back to the breakfast-room, opening the door gingerly as she peered anxiously at him, now seated in an easy-seat to one side of the large bay window. 'What's wrong?' She spoke directly to Dr Lambeth as he turned to face her. 'Is he all right?'

'No.' Her father's friend's voice was flat. 'No, he isn't, I'm afraid, Katie. I've been warning him for months to get checked out but due to his own particular brand of bullheadedness he refused to listen to me. I'm going to call an ambulance.'

'No way.' Her father was as white as a sheet and his voice was a mere whisper of its normal, steel-like quality but his face was as determined as ever. 'If I have to go to that damn hospital, I'll go in your car, Mark.'

'You won't.' Even as her father spoke Mark Lambeth lifted the extension at his elbow. 'I'm not being responsible for your having another attack on the way, David, and that's final. There is equipment in the ambulance that you might need. Now don't be such a damn fool. If you are too stubborn to think of yourself, think of your daughters, man.'

'Dad?' Katie's eyes were wide as she stared down at the man whom she had always considered as unmovable as the Rock of Gibraltar. Her father was never ill; she couldn't remember him ever being less than one hundred per cent fit in the whole of her life. In fact, he looked on even the most severe illness as a weakness that was easily banished through sheer self-will, and was scathing with those lesser mortals about him when they couldn't accomplish what he apparently found easy to do. 'Dad, what's wrong?'

'It's his heart, Katie.' Mark Lambeth answered again, and it was in that instant that Katie realised how serious things were. Her father wouldn't have tolerated being side-stepped in the normal run of things and Mark, old friend that he was, wouldn't have attempted it. 'He's had several warnings and now—' He stopped abruptly at the look of horror on Katie's face. 'Now he will have to come into hospital,' he finished flatly.

The ambulance was on the doorstep within four minutes and her father totally refused to let anyone but Mark ac-company him to the hospital. It hurt, but he had been hurt-ing her all his life and, if Katie hadn't exactly got used to it, she had learnt how to endure it without letting her feel-ings show.

She stared for some minutes down the long, wind-swept drive after the ambulance had departed, her thoughts in turmoil, before turning and re-entering the house where Mrs Jenkins was hovering anxiously in the hall. 'Oh, Katie, I can't believe it.' The small woman was nearly crying as she wrung her hands helplessly. 'Not Mr David.'

'He'll be all right, Mrs Jenkins.' Katie reached out and hugged the woman she had known most of her life and who had been something of a substitute mother since Ka-tie's own mother had died when she was ten. 'You know Dad; he's as strong as an ox.'

'Yes, he is, isn't he?' Mrs Jenkins swallowed deeply and made for the kitchen. 'I'll fix us both a strong cup of coffee and then we'd better try to contact Jennifer. Do you know where she is?'

'On an assignment in Monte Carlo, I think, but the paper will have her number,' Katie said flatly as Mrs Jenkins' words reminded her of the telephone call of ten minutes ago. Carlton Reef. She'd have to phone him and explain somehow. He surely wouldn't expect her father to phone him from the hospital, would he? She recalled the hard, cold male voice and the barely controlled rage evident in every word, and shivered helplessly. But then again...

It took her nearly ten minutes to find his number in her father's address book on his desk in his study due to the fact that it was under a firm's name rather than his own. 'Tone Organisation. Chairman and Managing Director, Carlton Reef,' she said thoughtfully as she read the scrawly handwriting.

She had been sipping Mrs Jenkins' scalding hot coffee as she hunted and it had had the effect of stilling the trembling in her limbs and calming her racing heartbeat a little. In spite of her brave words to the housekeeper she was desperately afraid for her father, and the suddenness of it all still made her faintly nauseous as she made the call.

'Tone Organisation. Can I help you?' As the uninterested voice of the telephonist came on the line Katie took a deep breath and forced herself to speak quietly and coolly.

'Can I speak to Mr Reef, please?' she said politely. 'He is expecting the call.'

'I'll put you through to his secretary.'

A few more seconds elapsed and then a cultured, beautifully modulated female voice spoke silkily. 'Mr Reef's office. Can I help you?'

As Katie gave her name and a brief explanation to the disembodied voice she felt her stomach tighten in anticipation of what was to come, and it was with a sense of anticlimax that she heard the secretary's voice speak again a minute or so later. 'I'm sorry, Miss White, I understand that Mr Reef was expecting your father to call.' It was said pleasantly enough but with just the faintest condemnation in the soft tones. 'He really can't spare the time—'

'My father has been taken into hospital,' Katie said tightly as she felt her face begin to burn with impotent anger. 'I'm fully aware of what Mr Reef was expecting but he'll have to make do with me, I'm afraid.'

'Just a moment.' There were a few more seconds of silence and then the secretary spoke again, her voice faintly embarrassed now. 'I'm sorry, Miss White, but Mr Reef said he did make it plain to you that it is your father he needs to contact. He doesn't think there is any point in talking to you.'

'Now just a darn minute.' Katie fairly spat the words down the phone. 'My father has been rushed to hospital with a heart attack and that creep you work for hasn't even got the decency to *talk* to me? Whatever he is paying you, it isn't enough for working for a low-life like him.'

'Miss White——'

'Look, this isn't your fault but I see no purpose in continuing this conversation,' Katie said stiffly before slamming the phone down so hard that the small table quivered under the force of it.

The pig! The arrogant, cold, supercilious pig! She tried to take a sip of coffee but her hands were shaking so much that she couldn't lift the cup, which made her still angrier. A combination of shock at her father's sudden collapse and rage at Carlton Reef's total lack of sympathy brought the tears she had kept at bay so far burning hot into the back of her eyes. She sat for long minutes trembling with the strength of her emotions before she wiped her wet eyes with a resolute hand and dialled the number of the local hospital with her heart in her mouth.

She was put through almost immediately to Mark whose calm, unflappable voice reassured her somewhat. 'It's as I expected, Katie,' the doctor said gently. 'His heart is struggling a little—I've recognised it for some time—but with certain medication or perhaps even an operation he can carry on more or less as normal.'

'Did he have a heart attack?' she asked nervously.

'I won't lie to you, Katie; you're over twenty-one and well able to take the rough with the smooth from what I've seen of you. Yes, it was a heart attack. He's all wired up at the moment and the results aren't too good but they're far from fatal, so don't let your imagination run riot. He's been working too hard of late but you can't tell him. At sixty he's no spring chicken.'

'No...' She smiled shakily. 'Can I come and see him?'

'Leave it for now,' he said gently. 'He'd hate you to see him at the moment; you know how he is.'

Yes, she knew how he was, Katie thought painfully as the shaft of agony that whipped through her body made her gasp. If it had been Jennifer here he would have allowed her to see him, but the simple fact was that he didn't rate his younger daughter at all. She shut her eyes tight and forced her voice to remain normal. 'But he's in no danger?' she asked quietly.

'Not now.' Mark's voice was soothing. 'I only wish I could have got him in here months ago.'

'Thank you, Doctor.' She could feel the tears bubbling to the surface and knew she had to finish the call quickly. 'I'll phone later, if I may?'

'Of course. Goodbye, Katie.'

'Goodbye, and thank you.'

She sat for long minutes in the overwhelmingly male study before wiping her eyes for the second time, phoning a local taxi firm and checking the address of the Tone Organisation in her father's smart address book. Somehow, during that telephone call with Dr Lambeth, something that had been forming slowly through the last few years of her life crystallised in her mind.

She was aware that her father treated her with an off-hand, almost casual and often slightly caustic tolerance that was totally absent from his dealing with her older sister. Jennifer had chosen a career in the cut-and-thrust, dog-eat-dog world of journalism and was doing wonderfully well. This her father could both understand and respect. Whereas she…

She blinked as she laid the book down on the desk. She had chosen to work with physically handicapped children in a local school after finishing her degree at university, despite better, more up-market job offers. The hours were long, the salary low and the mental and physical exhaustion that were part of the job sometimes seemed too much to bear but the rewards… She straightened her back as she stood up. The rewards as the children under her care learnt to live to their potential were enormous and something that her father would never understand, she thought painfully.

'Where are you going, Katie—the hospital?' Mrs Jenkins met her in the hall as the taxi driver rang the bell. Katie's neat red Fiesta was sitting in the drive but she knew she was in no fit state to drive herself.

'No.' She smiled as she answered although it was an effort. 'Dad doesn't want any visitors although Dr Lambeth said he isn't in any danger.'

'Thank goodness.' Mrs Jenkins shut her eyes for a moment and then smiled mistily at her. 'I told you, didn't I?'

'Of course you did.' Katie smiled back at the homely face she had come to love over the years. 'I have to sort out some business affair of Dad's—you know, that other phone call? It's urgent and I can't really leave it but if anyone should phone you know nothing about it. OK?'

'Of course, my dear.' Mrs Jenkins understood her perfectly. 'Anyone' meant one person and one person only. 'I wouldn't say a word. We just want him to get better, don't we?'

Their house was situated on the outskirts of London, in a pleasant suburb with gracious tree-lined avenues and large houses in their own immaculate grounds. As the taxi ate up the miles into the capital the general vista changed to miles and miles of identical terraced dwellings, rows of shops broken only by the odd garage and, eventually, blocks of office buildings, neutral and blank in the cool March air.

The taxi stopped at a particularly imposing high-rise monstrosity and she saw the sign, 'Tone Organisation', with a little quiver of her nerves. But she wasn't backing out now. Her father might not think much of her but that didn't matter. This was something that needed to be done; Carlton Reef had made that plain. It wouldn't just go away—or, rather, *he* wouldn't just go away, she corrected grimly as she stared up at the tall building.

She needed to buy her father some time. She stuck out her small chin aggressively and leant forward to the driver. 'Could you wait?' she asked firmly. 'I shan't be long.'

'No problem, miss.' She received a toothy grin. 'You're paying.'

The offices were busy and full but by the time the smart lift had carried her up to the top floor all was hushed opulence and quiet elegance. She found the secretary's office with no trouble and prepared for battle as she opened the door, but the office was empty, the interconnecting door with the office on the left partly open.

'I don't care what it takes.' She knew that voice, she thought blindly as her stomach dropped into her feet. 'This is one hell of a mess, Robert, and you do what you can to get us out of it. Get back to me.' The sound of a receiver being banged down made her flinch but in the next instant the doorway was full of a big male body and a hard square face was staring at her with something akin to amazement in the narrowed eyes. 'Who the hell are you?'

She realised that she wasn't dressed in office mode, but the worn denims and thick jumper that she had donned that morning were ideal for her work, as was the no-nonsense hairstyle that held her long honey-blonde hair in a severe

French plait at the back of her head. But in this world of pencil-slim skirts and the latest designer suits she was sadly out of place.

She lifted her chin a fraction higher and stared straight into the piercing grey eyes that were watching her so intently. 'I'm Katie White, Mr Reef, and I want a word with you.' She was glad her voice didn't betray her—inside she was a mass of quivering jelly. 'I have to say you are, without exception, the rudest, most objectionable man I have ever had the misfortune to come into contact with. My father is in Intensive Care at the moment with a heart attack—not that I expect you to be interested in that—and other than wheel the bed down here I had no alternative but to come here myself, as you wouldn't accept my call.'

'How did you get past Reception and my secretary?' he asked grimly, without the flicker of an eyelash.

There was something in the complete lack of response to her tirade that was more daunting than any show of rage but she forced herself not to wilt as she continued to face him. 'Reception was busy; a party of Japanese businessmen had just arrived,' she answered shortly. 'So I just slipped into the lift once I'd found your name and floor on the notice-board. And your secretary—' she glanced round the large room with her eyebrows raised '—is your problem, not mine.'

'I see.' He continued to survey her from the doorway and she was forced to acknowledge, albeit silently, that he really was the most formidable man she had seen for a long, long time. He was tall, very tall, with a severe haircut that held his black hair close to his head and accentuated the hard, aggressive male features even more. He could have been any age from thirty to forty—the big lean body was certainly giving nothing away—but the overall air of control and authority suggested that he had learnt plenty in the school of life.

'Well, Miss White, now you're here I suggest you come and sit down so we can discuss this thing rationally,' he said smoothly, after several seconds had passed in complete silence. 'You're obviously upset and I would prefer the dirty linen to be kept under wraps, as it were.'

'I couldn't care less about your dirty linen,' she shot back furiously, incensed beyond measure as he shook his dark head lazily, a mocking smile curving the full, sensual lips for a brief moment.

'I was referring to yours, not mine,' he said laconically. 'Or, to be more precise, your father's.'

'Now look here—'

'No, you look here, Miss White.' Suddenly the relaxed façade was gone and the man standing in front of her was frightening. 'You force your way into my office unannounced, breathing fire and damnation, when, by rights, it should be me squealing like a stuck pig.' He eyed her furiously. 'I'm sorry to hear that your father has had a heart attack, if in fact that is the case,' he added cynically, 'but that is absolutely nothing to do with me. The loss of a good deal of money and, more importantly, Miss White, my business credibility is, however, *everything* to do with *him*.'

'I don't know what you mean.' She had taken a step backwards without realising it and now, as he stared into the big hazel eyes watching him so fearfully, Carlton Reef forced himself to draw on his considerable store of self-control before he spoke again.

'Then let me explain it to you. Shall we?' He indicated his office with a wave of his hand, standing back from the doorway and allowing her to precede him into the room.

'How much do you know of your father's business affairs, Miss White?' he asked her quietly, once she was seated in the chair facing the massive polished desk behind which he sat.

'Nothing,' she answered honestly. 'My father—' She

stopped abruptly. 'He isn't the sort of man to talk about business at home,' she finished flatly. Or, at least, not to her, she amended silently. Never to her.

'And this heart attack?' He eyed her expressionlessly. 'It's genuine?'

'Of course it's genuine,' she answered in horror. 'What on earth do you think——?' She shook her head blindly as words failed her. 'No one would make something like that up,' she finished hotly.

'You'd be surprised,' he said sardonically. 'When the chips are down most people would do just about anything.'

'Well, I wouldn't.' She glared at him fiercely. 'You can ring the hospital if you like and speak to Dr Lambeth, my father's friend. I presume you would trust a doctor at least?' she finished scathingly.

'I trust very few people, Miss White.' He shifted slightly in the big leather chair, leaning back and surveying her through narrowed grey eyes.

'Like my father.' The words were condemning and he recognised them as such.

'You don't approve?' he said mildly. 'You're an optimist, Miss White—a very dangerous thing to be in the business world.'

'Well, as I'm not in the business world I wouldn't lose too much sleep over it,' she replied carefully. 'And I wouldn't describe myself as an optimist anyway; I just think most people verge on kindness given a chance.'

He shut his eyes for a split-second as he shook his dark head slowly, the gesture more eloquent than any words, and then opened them to stare directly into the greeny-brown of hers. 'What world *are* you in?' he asked quietly, his eyes wandering over the pale creamy skin of her face and stopping for an infinitesimal moment on her wide, generous mouth. 'You do work for a living?'

'Yes.' She straightened a little in the chair as she rebelled against the questioning. 'But I don't see how that affects why I'm here today, Mr Reef. You said on the phone that my father had lost you some money…?'

'Lost me some money?' he repeated sarcastically. 'Well, that's one way of putting it, I guess. A little oversimplified but nevertheless… Have you read the morning papers?' he asked abruptly.

'The morning—?' She hesitated at the change of direction. 'No—no, I haven't. My father was reading them when he—' She stopped again. 'When he collapsed,' she finished flatly.

'They nearly had the same effect on me,' he said drily, and then shook his head at her outraged expression. 'And I wasn't belittling your father's condition, Miss White. Here—' He thrust a newspaper at her abruptly. 'Read that.'

She glanced at where he was pointing but the black letters were dancing all over the page as she tried to read them and she looked up after a moment, her eyes enormous in her white face. 'I'm sorry, I can't take anything in.'

'It's the total collapse of a certain economy that your father assured me was one hundred per cent solid,' he said coolly. 'I have invested a vast amount of money at his persuasion and within the last few months, too. I've been made to look ridiculous, Miss White, and I can't say it appeals.'

'But—' she stared at him desperately '—he wouldn't have done it on purpose, would he? No one's perfect.'

'"No one's"—?' He held her eyes for several seconds before shaking his head again. 'This whole morning is fast beginning to resemble *Alice Through the Looking Glass*.'

A movement in the outer office caught his eye and he pressed the buzzer on his desk as he glanced towards the door. A second or two later, one beautifully coiffured head appeared round the door. 'I'm sorry, Mr Reef, I had to…'

The well-bred voice died as the woman glanced in Katie's direction.

'Two coffees, please, Jacqueline, and hold all calls,' Carlton Reef said quietly.

'Oh, but I can't—' Katie glanced at him as he raised enquiring eyebrows. 'I've got a taxi waiting for me in the street. I can't—'

'Pay it off, Jacqueline.' He settled further into his seat as he raised one hand thoughtfully under his chin. 'And phone... What hospital is your father in?' he asked Katie abruptly. She told him quietly as her cheeks burnt scarlet. He thought she was lying; how *could* he think that? 'Tell them I want to speak to a Dr Lambeth,' he instructed his secretary quietly, 'and do it discreetly, there's a good girl.'

It was the first time that Katie had been able to examine him without having his piercing grey eyes trained on her and as she looked at him, really looked at him for the first time, she had to admit in a tiny, detached part of her brain that he really was devastatingly good-looking in a hard, macho sort of way.

His skin was dark, with the sort of even tan that suggested a recent holiday somewhere very hot and very expensive, and the dark grey eyes were fringed with short jet-black lashes under heavy dark brows. Big, broad shoulders suggested an impressive body under the beautifully cut suit and she had already seen that he was tall—well over six feet. And he was as hard as iron. She stiffened as the razor-sharp eyes switched back to her. He was the sort of man her father would respect and admire and whom she loathed.

'Now—' he didn't smile as the secretary shut the door without a sound and they were left alone '—why exactly did you feel it necessary to come here?'

'You phoned.' She stared at him with a mixture of bewilderment and anger. 'You made it clear that my father would be in some sort of trouble if he didn't—'

'He's in deep trouble already, Miss White, and I'm afraid there is nothing you can do about it.' There wasn't a trace of compassion in the deep voice and she knew, as she stared into the implacable, cold features, actual hate for another human being for the first time in her life. 'I am not sure of my facts yet, so I do not intend to say much more, but from the little I do know about this unfortunate episode it would seem to suggest that your father did not do the homework he was paid to do. Supposition is not an option in the market-place and for this to happen without any prior warning...' He shrugged eloquently. 'Something smells.'

'Are you saying that my father was dishonest?' she asked hotly. 'Because if you are—'

The buzzer on his desk interrupted further conversation and, as he took the call his secretary had put through, his face was blank and composed. It was obviously from Dr Lambeth and by the time he replaced the receiver, some minutes later, the dark face was thoughtful, although she had been unable to comprehend anything from his side of the conversation. As he finished the call his secretary knocked quietly and entered with the coffee, her face smooth and expressionless.

'Thank you, Jacqueline.' He glanced up once, busying himself with the tray. 'Can you arrange for the car to be brought to the main entrance in ten minutes, please?'

'Yes, Mr Reef.'

Something had been said during that phone call, something disturbing and relevant to her, Katie thought suddenly as she stared into the cool poker face opposite. 'Is my father all right?' she asked quietly. 'He isn't worse?'

'No.' He handed her a cup of coffee and gestured towards the milk and sugar. 'Help yourself.'

'What did Dr Lambeth say?' she persisted, the trickle of unease gathering steam by the second. 'There's something you're not telling me, I know it.'

He stared at her for a good fifteen seconds before replying and she knew she was right. There *was* something— she could read it in the opaque blankness of his eyes. 'This is really nothing to do with me,' he said quietly. 'I feel it would be better if your father's friend explained in the circumstances, Miss White.'

'What circumstances?' She could feel her voice rising but there was nothing she could do about it as sheer undiluted panic gripped her insides. 'He's worse? He's not...' She stared at him with huge eyes.

'No, nothing like that.' He waved his hand at her almost irritably. 'I'm satisfied that whatever your father did he did out of ignorance, incidentally. Not that that makes the results any different but—' He stopped abruptly. 'Why the hell did you have to come here today anyway?' he growled savagely.

'Why?' She glared at him, more angry than she could remember being in her whole life. 'Because you threatened me, that's why. You said—'

'I know what I said.' He stood up in one sharp movement and walked over to the huge plate-glass window where he stood with his back to her, looking down on the ant-like creatures below in the busy London street. 'I just didn't expect you to come here hotfoot like some guardian angel, that's all.'

'Well, all that could have been averted if you'd taken my call,' she said stiffly as her face burned still more. He was a monster, she thought, an absolute monster.

'Possibly.' He still didn't turn round. 'Well, perhaps the news would be better coming from a stranger, after all. I don't know. At least you would have some time to prepare yourself.'

'Mr Reef, you're frightening me,' she said in a very small voice and, at that, he did turn, swinging round to see her sitting on the edge of her chair, hands clasped together and face as white as a sheet. 'Whatever it is—could you just tell me?' she asked slowly.

'Your father is bankrupt.' He had taken a deep breath before he spoke but the smoky grey eyes didn't leave her face. 'He's lost the business, the house, the cars, every penny he owns in this deal. He's just unburdened himself to Dr Lambeth and asked him to let all interested parties know.'

All interested parties? Somehow that hurt more than anything else could have done. She lived at home, spoke to him every day, shared little moments of his life and he hadn't even hinted that things were bad. What had she ever done that her own father disliked her so much, trusted her so little? What sort of person did he think she was?

'Miss White, did you hear me?' He moved round the desk to stand in front of her, before kneeling and bringing his face into line with hers. 'He had suspected the worst for days but seeing it in black and white in the newspaper brought the heart attack on, so I understand. The house is mortgaged up to the hilt, there are debts mounting sky-high—'

'I understand.' She stopped him with a tiny wave of her hand as she spoke through stiff lips. 'And he bore all this alone; he didn't say a word to anyone.'

'He's a businessman, Katie.' She wasn't aware that he had spoken her name as her mind struggled to comprehend what he had told her. Their beautiful home that had been in her father's family for generations... The loss of that alone would kill him, she knew it. 'He has to make decisions that are sometimes difficult—'

'He's my *father*.' She raised her head to stare at him, her eyes drowning in the whiteness of her face. 'He should have been able to talk about it with me. What else are families for if not to share the hard times? If he could have told me, trusted me, he might not be in hospital now connected to a mass of wires and tubes—'

She wasn't aware that her voice had risen into a shrill shriek, but when the outer door burst open and the secretary rushed in she was conscious of a stinging slap across her face as Carlton Reef pulled her back from hysteria before lifting her body into his arms and signalling for the woman to leave with a sharp movement of his head.

'It's all right; shush now, shush…' He was sitting in the chair she had been occupying with her cradled on his lap as she moaned her anguish out loud, the hopelessness of endless years of trying to win her father's love and approval culminating in the devastating knowledge that he could have died and she wouldn't have known why. He hadn't wanted her, hadn't reached out, hadn't needed even a word of comfort from the daughter he seemed to despise so much.

'Why didn't he *tell* me?' she asked again, her head buried in the folds of his jacket. 'He should have *told* me.'

'He didn't want to worry you,' Carlton said comfortingly, somewhere over her head. 'That's natural in a father.'

'No.' She struggled away from him as she desperately tried to compose herself, suddenly horrified at the position she had put herself in. There was nothing natural about her father but she couldn't tell this man that—he wouldn't understand. She had never known her father share the smallest thing with her, never felt a fatherly hug, never had anyone to dry her tears as all her friends had. 'You wouldn't understand,' she said weakly. 'I'm sorry; I shouldn't have come. I didn't know—'

'Look, sit down and have your coffee.' He had risen as she had moved away and now took her arm gently, pushing her back down in the seat as he passed a cup to her. 'Drink that and then I'll run you home. It's been a tremendous shock for you.'

'I don't want it.' She stood up again and faced him, her face drawn and pale. 'And I'll make my own way home, Mr Reef.' She felt as if she could die of embarrassment at the ridiculous picture she made. Here she was, in the very centre of the hive that made up London's busy business world, behaving like some brainless schoolgirl. What on earth was he thinking and why, oh, why, had she come? She must have been mad, quite mad, but she hadn't been thinking straight. In fact, she hadn't been thinking at all!

She bit her lower lip hard. She'd made a bad situation wellnigh impossible. 'I'm sorry about all this,' she said stiffly to the hard, handsome face watching her so intently. 'I thought that if I came to see you and explained that my father was ill you would be able to wait a few days, that things could be sorted...' Her voice trailed away at the expression on his face. If cynical mockery could go hand in hand with reluctant sympathy then that was what she was seeing.

'And instead you found the very roof over your head was threatened,' he intervened softly. 'I do understand your predicament, Miss White. I'm not quite such an ogre as you seem to think.'

'No?' She faced him square-on now, a combination of shock and crucifyingly painful hurt making her speak her mind in a way she would never have done normally. 'Well, as you've pointed out, our worlds are very different, Mr Reef, and your standards and those of my father are not mine. The lust for power and wealth that masquerades as ambition is not for me.'

'I see.' His face had closed against her as she had spoken and now his mouth was grim. 'But, unless I am very much mistaken, you have enjoyed the benefits of this world that you seem to despise so much for a good many years without your conscience being *too* troubled?' His eyebrows rose mockingly. 'Or perhaps you live in a little wooden hut at the end of your father's property and indulge in hair-shirts and a monastic form of life?'

'Of course I don't.' Amazingly the confrontation was making her feel better, quelling the panic and fear that had gripped her since he had told her of their changed circumstances as fierce anger at his mockery left no room for any other emotion. 'And I am grateful to my father for all he's done for me—my education, our home, all the "benefits" you could no doubt list as well as I could. But—' she raised her chin and the large, clear hazel eyes that stared into his were steady '—I can manage without them without it being the end of the world. I don't *need* them in the same way that you do, Mr Reef.'

'Don't you indeed?' His face was dark with an emotion she'd rather not dwell on now, and he crossed his arms as he leant back against the window, almost as though he needed to keep them anchored to his body rather than round her neck, she reflected silently. 'And how do you know what *I* need, Miss White? To my knowledge we have never met before today.'

'I know your type.'

'*My "type"*?' he barked angrily. 'My—' He broke off as he fought visibly for control before taking a deep breath and laughing harshly, the sound grating in the quiet air. 'You really do take the biscuit! You barge your way in here, flinging insults around as though they were confetti and then accuse me—'

He broke off again and shook his head before turning from her so that his hard features were in profile. 'You've had a bad day and I would guess that it's going to get worse. Let's leave it at that, and despite the low opinion you obviously have of me, I would not dream of letting you find your own way home after the news I've just given you. The car will be outside now. Shall we?'

He turned and extended his hand to the door. She remained staring at him for one long moment before she moved forward. He was angry, very angry; that much she could see and she really couldn't take on any more now. It was simpler to accept this favour, however much it grated.

'Mr Reef?' His secretary's voice held a note of panic as he walked with Katie through the outer office, shrugging his big grey overcoat over his shoulders as he did so. 'You haven't forgotten the management meeting you called earlier? They're already assembling in the small boardroom—'

'Cancel it.' Her employer turned at the door to fix her with that cool gaze. 'Re-schedule for two this afternoon.'

'Is there a number where you can be reached?'

'No—' he was already shutting the door as he replied to the slightly dazed voice '—but I won't be long.'

'You don't have to do this.' As the silent lift sped swiftly downwards she ventured a glance at him through her eyelashes and then wished she hadn't. He looked mad—more than mad, she thought weakly, and she hadn't fully realised just how big and powerful that tall, lean body was until the close confines of the lift had emphasised it so threateningly. And his aftershave was gorgeous...

What was she *doing*, thinking such things at a time like this? she asked herself faintly, and about a man like him, too—the sort that populated her father's world in droves and the kind she had always abhorred. She was in shock. She leant limply against the wall of the lift and took a long, silent breath. That was it. That had to be it. Either that or she'd lost it completely.

He had ignored her hesitant voice as though he hadn't heard it but now the cold grey eyes pierced her, the expression in them anything but friendly. 'You aren't going to faint on me, are you,' he asked grimly, 'on top of everything else?'

'No, I'm not.' The adrenalin that sent fierce colour into

her cheeks and an angry sparkle into her eyes also brought her jerking off the lift wall to stand rigid and stiff as they reached the ground floor. 'I've never fainted in my life.'

'Quite a formidable lady.' The thread of laughter in the mocking voice was unforgivable in the circumstances, and sheer anger kept her head up and her back straight as they walked through the reception area.

Out of the corner of her eye she was aware of one or two interested but veiled glances in their direciton, but just keeping up with his large strides was more than enough to contend with for the moment. She had absolutely no intention of following in his wake like a whipped puppy, she thought tightly as they reached the massive automatic doors together. He was the epitome of the arrogant, dominant male but the Tarzan-Jane concept of male and female had never appealed less than at this moment.

The icy March wind was carrying chips of sleet on its breath as they left the hothouse warmth of the big building and she pulled her knee-length anorak more tightly round her as a big dark blue Mercedes purred to a halt in front of them, complete with chauffeur in matching uniform.

'In you get.' He opened the door for her and then followed her into the immaculate interior in one movement. 'Your address?' She gave it in a small voice that tried to be cool and assured but was merely...small.

'Are you going to the hospital?' They had travelled some minutes in complete silence but she had never been more aware of another human being in her life.

'Later perhaps.' Why couldn't he have been old and bald? she asked herself as she turned her head to meet his gaze. A sympathetic uncle-figure who would have met her halfway? 'My father doesn't—' She corrected herself quickly. 'The doctor thought it better to keep him quiet for the moment.'

'Right.' The intuitive grey eyes had narrowed at the slip

but he made no comment, his face bland, and he turned to look out of the window into the grey world outside as the big car moved swiftly through the mid-morning traffic.

The journey home was accomplished in about half the time the taxi had taken earlier and as they drew into the smart pebbled drive she found herself looking, as though for the first time, at the house she had been born in. Mellow, honey-coloured stone, leaded windows and a massive thatched roof stared impassively back; the huge oak tree that stood in the middle of the bowling-green-smooth lawn at the front of the house was as yet bare and naked against the winter sky.

'You have a beautiful home.' She jumped visibly as he spoke, and dragged her eyes away from the sight that had suddenly become so poignant with a tremendous effort.

'Not for much longer, it would seem,' she said flatly as she held out one small, slim hand for him to shake. 'Thank you for bringing me home, Mr Reef. No doubt my father's solicitors will be hearing from yours in due course.'

'No doubt.' He hesitated for the merest second and then, instead of giving the handshake she had expected, leant forward and brushed her lips with his own. As she leapt backwards like a scalded cat he climbed out of the car and offered his hand, his eyebrows raised in a distinctly sardonic tilt. 'Allow me.'

She gave him her hand reluctantly—a fact which the dark eyebrows took full note of—and slid out of the car with as much dignity as she could muster, considering her cheeks were glowing bright red and her mouth was burning from the brief contact with his.

'Goodbye,' she said again, a little breathlessly this time, as she stepped backwards a few paces from his large bulk and edged towards the house.

'Goodbye.' He didn't smile or move and after a split-second of indecision she turned and ran up the steps to the front door, her only desire being to get into the safety of the house.

Mrs Jenkins must have heard the car because even as she fumbled in her bag for her key the door opened and she almost fell into the hall in her eagerness to get inside. 'Katie?' Mrs Jenkins peered out into the drive before slowly shutting the door and hurrying to her side. 'Who was that man?' she asked worriedly. 'And why was he looking at the house like that?'

'Like what?' Katie asked weakly, the relief at being home overwhelming. She didn't know why but during the last few seconds in the car she had felt undeniably threatened—terrifyingly so.

'Like...' Mrs Jenkins' voice faded away as she shook her grey head bewilderedly. 'I don't rightly know, but it wasn't normal.'

'He's not a normal man, Mrs Jenkins,' Katie said unsteadily just as the phone began to ring. It was the first of many calls that day from her father's colleagues and business contacts who were already beginning to demand their pound of flesh.

CHAPTER TWO

'KATIE?' Her sister's voice was more irritated than concerned when they finally managed to contact her in her hotel in Monte Carlo later that afternoon. 'What's all this about Dad being taken ill? He's never been ill in his life.'

'Well, he is now,' Katie said quietly, carefully keeping any trace of emotion out of her voice.

Jennifer was a duplicate of their father temperament-wise, scorning any show of sentiment or warmth, single-minded when it came to her career as a top reporter for one of the national tabloids, and utterly ruthless when it came to having her own way. At twenty-eight, she was five years older than Katie and well able to afford a luxurious flat in the heart of London, her own expensive sports car and a wardrobe of up-to-the-minute clothes that she changed like her nail varnish.

'It's his heart.'

'His heart?' Her sister's voice was scornful. 'I didn't know he had one!'

'Jennifer!' Katie's voice expressed her outrage.

Jennifer and her father had always held a mutual respect for each other's inexorable character while recognising that they were too alike to get on if they saw much of each other. The sort of comment that Jennifer had just made was exactly the type her father would have given if the situation had been reversed, and neither would have taken umbrage, but just now... Just now she couldn't take it, Katie thought painfully.

Despite his wishes, she had been to see her father after lunch, stopping for just a minute or two and driving away shocked beyond measure at the change which had been wrought in him in just a few hours. He had been in a semi-doze, never really waking, and to see his strong, lean and powerful body still and lifeless under the clinical hospital sheets had hurt more than she would have thought possible.

'I'm sorry, Katie.' Jennifer's voice was impatient, which made the apology null and void. 'How is he, then?'

'Hard to say.' She wasn't going to make this easy for her, Katie thought with an uncharacteristic flare of anger—besides which, it was true. 'He had a heart attack this morning but then, just before I got there this afternoon, he had another one. Lambeth said he'll be OK once they get the medication balanced but, as in most things medical, nothing is for certain.'

'Oh.' She could tell the news wasn't to her sister's liking. 'Well, I've nearly finished here so I suppose I could fly in in the next day or two,' Jennifer said reluctantly.

'There's something else.' Katie took a deep breath in preparation for the explosion. 'Dad's bankrupt.'

'*What*?' Now she really had her attention, Katie thought grimly. 'What do you mean "bankrupt"? You're kidding me.'

'I'd hardly joke at a time like this,' Katie said quietly. 'He's mortgaged the house, the business and even the weekend cottage he bought for Mum originally, and there is an absolute mountain of debts. The cars, his boat, everything will have to go. I saw the solicitor this afternoon after I left the hospital.'

'Oh, brilliant, just brilliant.' Her sister's voice was scathing. 'What happened to the Midas touch he was always so proud of, then?'

'Well, I think he's paid for the loss of it, don't you?' Katie ground out through clenched teeth as she strove to keep her temper. 'It was the knowledge of how bad things were that brought on the heart attack.'

'Well, there's no room in my flat for anyone else,' Jennifer said quickly, after a moment's pause. 'I've got someone living in at the moment.'

'What's his name?' Katie asked tightly. Her sister was the original liberated woman, taking a new man into her life and her bed every few months and then kicking him out when she got bored, which was usually fairly quickly.

'Donald,' Jennifer drawled dispassionately. 'Hell, Katie, Dad'll hate the humiliation of bankruptcy, won't he? Not to mention losing the house. He really is a fool—'

'Don't you dare say that when you see him, Jen,' Katie hissed furiously. 'Not in words or one of those expressions you do so well. I'll murder you if you do.'

'Keep your hair on.' Her sister's voice was more amused than offended. 'Why you care so much about him I'll never know. You'll never learn, will you, Katie? You're just like Mum. Well, I've got to go, sweetie. I'll phone tomorrow and tell you what flight I'll be on. OK?'

'Goodbye, Jennifer.' Katie replaced the phone jerkily and strove for control. She should be hardened to it by now—she should, but her sister's total lack of emotion about anything but her precious job seemed to get harder to take as she grew older. And the casual reference to their mother... Katie could still remember the day she had died—the bleak, total despair and sense of loss that had never really dimmed through the years. She had learnt to live with the ache but had never really got over her mother's sudden death in a car accident when she was ten. They had been kindred spirits, totally different to look at but twin personalities and, in dark moments, Katie would still have given anything she possessed to gaze upon her face one more time and hug her tight.

It hadn't helped that her father and Jennifer had seemed almost unaffected either, although Katie had often thought, with her father at least, that it had been a way of coping with grief, to shut it in and refuse to acknowledge that it was there. But perhaps that was wishful thinking? She shook her head. Maybe Jennifer was right after all—she'd never learn, the eternal optimist always wanting to see the best in people. The thought brought the image of Carlton Reef into sudden focus before her eyes and she heard his scornful and derisive voice as though he were in the room with her.

'Right, enough is enough.' She rose determinedly from the chair. Tomorrow she would go into school, throw herself into the work there and face all the other mountains in her life when the time came. There was nothing she could do or say that would avert the catastrophe that had befallen them—it was far too late for that—but she was going to need to be strong for her father and herself.

How he would face the shame and humiliation she just didn't know; he was a fiercely proud man with unshakeable principles and this house in itself meant far more to him than mere collateral. Why on earth had he mortgaged it? She caught herself abruptly. No, recriminations were no good now; she needed to concentrate on the positive.

Over the next few days that resolution was to be sorely tested. News of the disaster travelled quickly in the business world and when she returned home from the school, often exhausted, the phone never seemed to stop ringing. Some of the callers were openly curious, digging for news, others faintly gloating that they themselves weren't in such dire straits; one or two were sympathetic and concerned and several verged on the abusive. The latter were mainly creditors who were doubting whether they would ever get paid.

Jennifer had called as promised, the day after her father's collapse, to say that the paper had contacted her shouting for a first-class reporter in France for a few days and would

Katie mind terribly if she just did that little job before she came home? Katie had replied that her sister must decide her own priorities and Jennifer had finished the call quickly, saying that she had to run as the plane to France was going to be a tight one to catch.

Altogether, as Katie made her way to the hospital on Friday night for her regular evening visit, four days after her father's collapse, she felt tired in mind and body and sick to her soul. Her father hadn't improved as Dr Lambeth had hoped. Indeed, he seemed faintly worse each day, as though the will to live was ebbing away, and, forcing a bright smile on her face as she walked into the small side-ward, she dreaded what she would find.

'Hello again.' The deep, cool voice hit her at the same moment that her numbed gaze took in the dark, lean body lazily seated at her father's side.

'*You*?' She barely glanced at her parent, all her energy concentrated on the hard, handsome face watching her so intently. What was he doing here? The answer was obvious—he'd come to badger a sick man. How dared he? How *dared* he?

'Not the most charming of greetings but it will have to do, I suppose.' And the creep was laughing at her. 'How are you, Katie?' he asked softly as he rose and offered her his chair.

'I think you ought to leave, Mr Reef.' She forced her voice to remain low but her eyes, daggers of steel aimed directly at his, spoke volumes. 'My father is a sick man and I won't have him upset.'

'*Katie!*'

She ignored her father's horrified exclamation and continued to look at the tanned face in front of her, which had lost its mocking amusement as though by magic. 'Did you hear me?' she asked tightly.

'I'm not here to upset your father, Katie,' Carlton said

coldly, 'although you seem to be doing a pretty good job of that yourself at the moment. Now would you please sit down and stop making a spectacle of yourself?' he finished coolly.

'Katie, for crying out loud...' Her father's agitated tones brought her eyes to his face for the first time and he nodded at the chair violently, his eyes lethal. 'Sit down, girl,' he barked angrily, more himself than he had been in days. 'Carlton is here purely as a friend, nothing more.'

'Really?' The word carried all the mistrust she felt for the man and her father shut his eyes for a moment in exasperation, shaking his head silently.

'Sit.' It was an order and she sat, but as Carlton moved another chair near the bed and stretched out his long legs to within an inch of hers it was all she could do to restrain the impulse to jerk away. She managed it—just. 'I'm sorry, Carlton.' David White waved his hand at her as he spoke. 'She isn't normally this way but my illness seems to have brought out the lioness-defending-her-cub mentality.'

'Not altogether a bad thing.' Carlton smiled back but, as the dark grey eyes moved to her, the smoky depths were as hard as iron. 'But the exterior doesn't quite prepare one for the fire and brimstone underneath.'

'Her mother was the same.' She glanced at him, utterly astounded as he spoke. She had never in all her life heard him compare her to his wife and it was still more amazing that his tone held a faint touch of embarrassed pride. 'She was sweetness personified, but if anyone threatened her family all hell was let loose. She was one special woman—'

He broke off, clearly horrified at having said so much, and there was a brief moment of charged silence before Carlton stepped into the breach. Katie was staring at her father open-mouthed, quite stunned. If a choir of heavenly angels had suddenly appeared in the room she couldn't have been more surprised.

Carlton glanced at Katie whose astounded countenance spoke for itself and then at David who was staring determinedly out of the window, his face ruddy with embarrassment, before shifting slightly in his seat and speaking in a cool, matter-of-fact voice that defused the awkward atmosphere.

'There are some papers in your father's study at home that might be important, Katie, and he'd like me to have a look through them in case there's a way out of this mess. Perhaps we could leave together and I could pick them up on the way home?'

'I'm in my own car,' she answered automatically as she dragged her eyes away from her father's stiff face with tremendous effort and turned to Carlton.

'No problem.' He smiled easily. 'I'll follow you home in mine. I'd really rather look at them as soon as possible. If anything's going to be done it's got to be quick.'

'You think there's a chance?' Katie asked quietly as she looked fully into the smoky grey eyes, receiving a slight jolt as the full power of the piercing gaze held hers.

'Possibly.' She couldn't read a thing from his face—it was a study in neutrality. 'From what David tells me, he was ill-advised himself and someone has certainly reaped a vast profit from this little deal. Now, whether it was actually illegal or not is another question and one that needs answering before the dust settles.'

'I see.' She didn't want him to come to her house; she didn't want anything at all to do with him, but in the face of what he was suggesting she had no choice but to smile, albeit painfully, and incline her head. 'Well, of course, if my father thinks you should investigate further—'

'I do.' David cut into the conversation sharply, his voice more alive than it had been for the last four days and certainly more full of energy than she had expected when she'd walked into the room that evening. 'Bankruptcy—'

He stopped abruptly. 'I've never owed anyone a penny in my life,' he continued gruffly, 'and it doesn't sit well, Katie, dammit! If there's a chance—'

'If there is I'll find it.' Carlton's voice was smooth as he spoke but there was some inflexion, just something she couldn't put a name to, that made Katie stare at him hard. He was so cold this man, so in control. She didn't trust him; she didn't trust him an inch, and she was suddenly more sure than ever that there was an ulterior motive governing what appeared to be a straightforward request.

'Dad, these papers...' She hesitated and searched for a way of disguising the question she had to ask. 'Are there any you'd prefer to keep confidential? I could bring them all in here tomorrow and let you sort through them with Mr Reef if that would be more helpful. You must know what you're looking for, after all, and he might miss—'

'No, no. Let Carlton take anything he needs, Katie,' David said briskly. 'He probably knows what he's looking for better than I do.'

She didn't doubt it, Katie thought grimly, and that was exactly what was bothering her. She stared helplessly at her father, willing him to read her mind and know what she was thinking but he just smiled back at her before turning to Carlton with an easy gesture of thanks. 'Anything you can do would be appreciated, Carlton.'

Anything he could do? She felt a little shiver of premonition as her father spoke. He had never made a mistake before in the business world that was his lifeblood; it seemed very strange that now, suddenly, he *had* made one, and one of such gigantic proportions that it would leave them totally destitute. Exactly what part had Carlton Reef played in all this? she wondered suspiciously. And why this offer of help now, after the rage of a few days ago?

As she turned to the dark figure at her side she realised, with a sudden surge of panic, that if her father had been unable to pick up the waves she was attempting to send him Carlton Reef had had no such problem. The grey eyes were chips of stone in an otherwise expressionless face, the mouth a taut, sardonic line of enquiry.

'I have a photocopier in my study at home, Miss White,' he said coolly, the use of her surname a distinct put-down. 'Would you like to accompany me there tonight so you can keep the originals in your possession?' It was a definite challenge and one, in view of her father's comments, that he didn't expect her to take up.

She stared at him for a few moments, her natural politeness and gentleness warring with the feeling that possessed her where this man was concerned. 'Yes, I would,' she said quietly, hearing David's exasperated indrawn breath with a resigned sense of the inevitable. He would disapprove of her actions in dealing with Carlton Reef in the same way he disapproved of everything but she wouldn't have been able to sleep tonight if she hadn't followed through on her instinct.

She knew, without a shadow of a doubt, that the astute, intelligent mind ticking away behind those hard grey eyes was several paces in front of theirs. Quite what he had in view she wasn't sure, but if she had had to answer the old 'friend or foe?' question there would have been no hesitation. Carlton Reef was no friend of theirs.

For the rest of the visit Katie sat quietly listening to the two men talk. Carlton didn't broach the business difficulties again, concentrating on light, witty conversation that kept David amused without him having to make any effort himself.

Carlton Reef was a formidable adversary, she thought silently as the minutes sped by. She had never met a man who generated such an air of easy authority, who seemed so totally sure of himself. And she was forced to recognise, after nearly an hour had passed, that, in spite of her distrust and dislike for the man, there was something compellingly attractive about him that was both fascinating and frightening.

She remembered the feel of being in his arms and that light kiss as he had left her a few days before and shivered in spite of the over-hot room. This was ridiculous, she told herself sternly. She needed to keep all her wits razor-sharp around him and thoughts of this nature were definitely out of order.

The smoky eyes turned to her as the round, clinical clock on the wall ticked to seven o'clock. 'Would you like a few minutes alone with your father, Katie?' he asked quietly. She noticed that he hadn't asked David and surmised that he had gleaned enough about their relationship to know what her father's reply would have been.

'Thank you.' She smiled stiffly. 'I won't be long.'

'There's really no need...' The older man's protest was lost as Carlton rose and leant across the bed to shake him by the hand, making his goodbyes as he did so.

'It'll probably take a few days to sift through the correspondence, David,' he said easily as he walked to the door after replacing the chair near the wall, 'but if there's anything I'll call you immediately after the solicitors have checked it out. OK?'

'Fine, fine.' Her father was beaming as the door closed and for a moment, as Katie glanced at him, she knew a dart of intense irritation. 'What's the matter?' As his eyes switched to her face she tried to relax her features but it was too late. 'You don't like him, do you? Why?' he asked disapprovingly.

'I don't know him,' she prevaricated quickly.

'He tells me you went to see him on the day I was brought in here,' he said quietly, 'after he'd phoned the house. That took some guts, Katie, but why didn't you tell me?'

'There was no need.' She forced a bright smile to her face as she wondered where the conversation was leading.

'Katie...' Her father hesitated and then leant back against the pillows, his face more drawn now that Carlton's stimulating company had left. 'The situation can't get worse than it is, now can it? If there's the faintest chance he can pull it round, even if it means we're left with the house and nothing else, it's worth a try. I got greedy, girl...'

She stared at him in absolute amazement for the second time in an hour, aware that they were having the first *real* conversation of their lives.

'I'd always planned to leave the house to you, you know. Jennifer would have been looked after with an equal financial payment but I've always seen my grandchildren being raised in the old home, somehow. I know that's what your mother would have liked. She was always so upset she hadn't produced a son to carry on the White name that she didn't realise all I wanted was her—'

He stopped abruptly and there was a moment of deep silence before he continued. 'I don't know why I mortgaged the house—it was a crazy thing to do—but I thought I was going to make a killing.' He smiled grimly. 'And there was a killing all right.'

'Don't think about it now, Dad.' She stood up quickly; the expression on his face was too painful to watch. 'You've got to concentrate on getting better.'

'I didn't want to before Carlton came today,' he said thoughtfully, his expression introspective, 'but if there is a chance...' He looked up, his face touchingly hopeful. 'You do see we have to take it?'

'Of course.' She bent to kiss him goodbye and he turned his cheek to her as normal, the gesture as aloof as always. On the rare occasions in the past when she had gathered her courage and tried to hug or kiss him the response had always been the same—this formal offering of his cheek

for a brief caress. 'Goodnight, Dad,' she said quietly, her
voice bleak. Nothing had altered, not really. No wonder he
liked Carlton so much. They were two of a kind—cold,
reserved men who gave nothing of themselves and wanted
no one.

Carlton was waiting for her just down the corridor, deep
in conversation with one of the doctors. 'Katie?' He looked
up as she carefully closed the door, and beckoned her to
them. 'There's a chance that your father might be allowed
home some time next week.'

'I understand you have a live-in housekeeper, Miss
White,' the young doctor said quietly. 'So he would have
someone with him at all times?'

'Yes.' She stared at him anxiously. 'You think he might
have another attack?'

'We hope not.' She received the standard reassuring
smile. 'But obviously he will take some time to recover
from this one, you do understand that?'

'Of course.'

'And rest and quiet are essential,' he continued briskly.
'So, we'll think again after the weekend and give you a
day or so's warning before he comes home.'

'Thank you.' As Carlton took her arm the doctor smiled
and left them, to enter the main ward on their right.

'Encouraging news?' Carlton said softly as they walked
towards the lift, his fingers burning her flesh as she strove
to remain calm and cool. She was vitally aware of him, his
touch, the timbre of his voice, and she allowed her head to
fall slightly forward so that the thick, silky fall of her hair
hid her face from his gaze.

'I suppose so.' There were several other people in the
lift and she relaxed slightly as it sped to the ground floor,
but once in the corridor leading to the car park she voiced
what was on her mind. 'But I'm hardly going to be able to

keep him quiet and calm with the house being sold over our heads and everything else that's going to happen.'

'Is there anywhere he could go while the worst of it takes place?' Carlton asked slowly. 'I understand your sister has a flat in London. Would she—?'

'No, she wouldn't,' Katie cut in flatly. 'The current boyfriend is in residence and, anyway, Jennifer is the last person to have her lifestyle interrupted in any way. She'd make my father miserable.' She shrugged. 'I'll think of something and perhaps, if you're successful, it won't be necessary anyway.'

'Right.' Again there was something, a slight inflexion in the bland voice, that made her glance at him sharply as they left the hospital.

'You meant what you said?' she persisted carefully as they walked down the path leading to the car park, a few thin flakes of wispy snow blowing in the icy wind. 'About trying to help?'

'Of course.' He stopped at the end of the path and turned to face her, his eyes veiled. 'It's in my own interest after all, isn't it? I do stand to lose as well by this deal, you know.'

'Some money, perhaps.' He seemed to tower over her as she looked up into his face, her honey-blonde hair blowing in silky tendrils over the satin-smooth skin of her face and her eyes huge in the dim light. 'But my father loses everything.'

'So do you.' His voice was very deep as his eyes followed the soft line of her mouth. 'But that has hardly occurred to you, has it?' There was a faint note of bewilderment in his voice but she was thinking about her father's face in those few minutes she had had alone with him and didn't notice.

'I have my work.' She looked up at him gravely. 'And I can find us a small flat somewhere but it will take time.

How long—?' She paused and then continued painfully. 'How long do these sorts of things take to happen?'

'Not long,' Carlton said expressionlessly. 'David has to declare himself bankrupt first and then things move fairly swiftly, I understand.'

'It'll kill him.' She looked over the cold, dark car park bleakly, her face desolate, and missed the sudden tightening of his mouth at her distress. 'Well...' she turned to him again and indicated her car some yards away '...that's my car, so if you want to follow...?'

'Fine.' He stood still for a brief moment, observing her quietly before striding over to the Mercedes, lost in the night shadows at the far side of the car park. She unlocked her door and slid into the car, starting the engine and turning on her lights as she waited for him to join her. The snow was falling a little more heavily now, big, flat flakes beginning to outnumber the tiny, thread-like ones of a few minutes ago. She normally found the sight entrancing but tonight her heart was too heavy for the normal elation.

As the powerful headlights of the Mercedes drew up behind her she pulled carefully out of the dark car park, the icy conditions and the fact that Carlton was just behind her making her unusually nervous. Stop it, Katie, she told herself sternly. You're a big girl now and you've been driving for years.

It didn't help.

The journey home through a world fast becoming a winter wonderland was uneventful and as she drew into the winding drive, grateful for the scrunchy pebbles under the car's wheels instead of the black ice she had encountered more than once on the main roads, her heart plummeted right into her boots. 'Jennifer.'

She pulled up at the side of her sister's expensive sports car and glanced back to where Carlton had just entered the drive. What was her sister going to make of all this? And, more importantly in the circumstances, what was Carlton going to make of her sister?

She wondered, for a split-second, if she had time to dash into the house and warn Jennifer to be on her best behaviour or at least be civil, but as Carlton unfolded his long body from the front of the car and slammed the door shut she resigned herself to the fact that it was too late.

She was fumbling with her key when he reached her side, and he gestured behind her to the car as the door swung open. 'That's my sister's car,' she said hurriedly as the warm, scented air from the hall reached out a welcome. 'She must have just arrived.'

'Better late than never,' Carlton murmured sardonically as he followed her into the house. 'Or perhaps in your sister's case that old cliché doesn't apply?' he added wickedly.

She didn't have time to reply. As they entered the house both Jennifer and Mrs Jenkins appeared from the drawing-room, the former cucumber-cool and as regal as ever and the latter clearly flustered.

'Darling…' Jennifer's beautiful almond-shaped blue eyes rested briefly on her sister before transferring to Carlton's hard, dark face, whereupon they brightened considerably. 'We've only just arrived, Katie,' she continued as she remained looking at Carlton, 'so there was no time to visit father tonight.'

'The visiting doesn't end till ten,' Katie said automatically, stiffening as another figure sauntered lazily out of the drawing-room.

'Oh, this is Donald,' Jennifer said in an aside over her shoulder. 'And *this* is…?' She held Carlton's impassive glance for a long moment before turning briefly to Katie. 'Aren't you going to introduce us to your friend, sweetie?'

'I…' Katie found herself at a loss for words and tried desperately to pull herself together. Why on earth had

Jennifer brought her current lover here now of all times? she thought helplessly. It had to be the worst possible timing.

Donald had come to a halt just behind her sister, resting a casual hand on her shoulder as he glanced nonchalantly in Katie's direction.

'You must be the little sister?' he drawled with a confidence that grated on Katie's nerves like barbed wire. 'Been holding the fort for Jennifer, then?' he added patronisingly.

'She's been doing a lot more than that.' Carlton's voice was crisp and clear and both Jennifer and her swain stiffened at the tone. 'And today has been a hard day like all the other ones before it, so might I suggest that we indulge in further niceties over a cup of coffee in the drawing-room?' The last part of the sentence he directed at Mrs Jenkins with a warm smile that had been totally absent when he had looked at Jennifer and Donald, and the small woman nodded quickly, her eyes grateful at his mastery of the situation.

'You go and sit down, my dear,' Mrs Jenkins said quickly as she glanced at Katie's drawn face. 'I'll bring it through in a minute.'

'Thank you, Mrs Jenkins.' Katie didn't know whether to be pleased or angry at Carlton's control over them all but it was simpler to be neither. 'I do feel exhausted tonight.'

'Poor darling.' Jennifer's voice was full of sweetness as they all walked through into the drawing-room but the hard blue eyes had difficulty in leaving Carlton's face for more than a few moments. She turned as Katie sank down into an easy-chair by the fire and held out her hand to Carlton, her eyes frankly appraising. 'I don't think we've met,' she said directly.

'I'm sure we haven't.' The mockery was back in Carlton's voice and his eyes were cool as they looked into the beautiful face in front of him. At twenty-eight, Jennifer was in the full bloom of her beauty and she knew it. There was no similarity between the two sisters except in the colour of their hair, but whereas Katie's was soft and wavy Jennifer's was cut into a sleek, expensive bob that framed the lovely heart-shaped face in which the clear, vivid blue eyes with their faintly oriental slant gave her a feline attractiveness that was infinitely seductive. 'I'm Carlton Reef,' he continued coolly. 'A friend of your father.'

'A business colleague,' Katie added from her armchair. 'Carlton has offered to look through Dad's papers and see if there is any way out of the mess we're in. He was involved in a considerable loss himself.'

'Oh, dear.' Jennifer reluctantly withdrew her hand as Carlton let go of hers. 'Not too bad, I hope?' she asked sweetly.

'I'll survive.' He glanced across at Donald who had been watching the little exchange with a faint frown on his good-looking face. 'You drove Jennifer down?' he asked pointedly.

'Not exactly.' Donald stiffened even as his eyes flickered beneath Carlton's icy gaze.

'Donald's a close friend of mine,' Jennifer said easily. 'Aren't you, darling? We thought it would be fun to have a few days out of the city together as I had to come down here anyway.'

'*Fun*?' Katie came back into the conversation with a vengeance as she saw red. 'You are supposed to be down here to see Dad, or had you forgotten?' she asked furiously. 'I hardly think "fun" comes into it!'

'Oh, don't be an old grouch,' Jennifer said with a total lack of heat, which told Katie that she had other fish to fry, and, as she watched her sister eat Carlton with her eyes, she had a good idea of what they might be. 'Donald can always take my car and disappear back to the flat, can't you, darling?' She glanced across at him and continued without waiting for an answer, 'And I'll stay here to help you, Katie.'

And pigs might fly, Katie thought balefully. She knew exactly what Jennifer had in mind—she had seen that predatory gleam in her sister's eyes before with more than one man. And she also knew the reason for the quick turn-about regarding Donald's visit. He would cramp her style if she were to indulge in a full-scale man-hunt.

'How sisterly.' Carlton's voice was bland, but as Jennifer's eyes returned to his face she saw the cynical mockery evident in every hard line and her mouth curved in a seductive little pout. This was the sort of man she both understood and appreciated.

'You don't mind going back tomorrow morning, do you, darling?' Jennifer turned to Donald with a languid wave of a limp hand. 'Perhaps it would be better with Father so ill.'

Donald obviously did mind, very much, but just as obviously he wasn't going to voice his protest with Carlton's piercing grey eyes trained on his face. He shrugged once, with a shake of his blond head, and said nothing but the pale blue eyes were malevolent.

As Mrs Jenkins bustled in with the coffee-tray the conversation came to a halt for a few moments, but once the housekeeper had left and everyone was seated Jennifer spoke directly to Carlton, her eyes curious. 'What exactly do you do, Mr Reef?' she asked sweetly.

'"Exactly"?' He was openly mocking her but she didn't seem to mind, Katie thought in amazement. She had never seen anyone treat her beautiful sister like this before; normally the boot was very definitely on the other foot. 'Well, "exactly" might take too long to explain,' he said easily, 'but among other interests I own the Tone Organisation. Perhaps you've heard of it?' he continued lightly as Jennifer's slanted eyes opened as wide as they could.

'I knew I recognised the name,' she breathed softly. 'I just knew it. You never told me,' she added accusingly to Katie who was watching the little by-play with some bewilderment.

'Told you what?' Katie asked in surprise.

'That you'd got *the* Carlton Reef down here,' her sister said breathlessly. 'I've been trying to fix up an interview with you for ages, you know,' she added as she turned the full hundred-watt smile in Carlton's direction. 'The paper has been doing a series on millionaires of the nineties. Perhaps you've read it?' she asked hopefully.

'I think not.' Carlton's voice was very dry.

'Oh.' Jennifer wasn't one to let a small put-down affect her. 'Well, your publicity department wasn't at all helpful,' she added with a faint touch of provocative helplessness. 'And it would mean *so* much to get a scoop at the moment.'

'Excuse me,' Katie interrupted as her stunned mind tried to make sense of what she had just heard. 'Are you telling me that you're a millionaire?' she asked Carlton flatly.

'I wasn't aware I was telling you anything.' His voice was guarded and very cool as he looked expressionlessly into her shocked face.

'But *are* you?' she persisted, still in the same flat voice.

'Do you mean to say you didn't know?' Jennifer laughed shrilly into the loaded atmosphere. 'Really, Katie, you live in a world of your own at that awful school. There is something beyond disinfectant and snotty noses, you know—'

'*Shut up.*' And for once in her life Jennifer did just that as her sister turned on her a glare that would have silenced Attila the Hun, before looking again into Carlton's dark face. 'What sort of man are you?' she hissed tightly as she rose slowly from her chair to stand over him like an avenging angel. 'To threaten my father like you did, to act as though the loss of that deal was the worst thing that had ever happened to you when all the time you're rolling in money...'

Carlton hadn't moved; in fact, neither had anyone else. The whole room had taken on the effect of a macabre tableau, frozen in time. 'He's lost everything—*everything*!' She could hardly get the words past her lips, so great was her fury. 'And you sit there like a big black spider with a hundred other webs, laughing at us!'

'I'm not laughing at you, Katie.' Carlton's voice was as flat as hers had been. 'And, if you remember, I thought your father had been...less than honest.'

'And that makes it all right?' she ground out through clenched teeth. 'To fool us—'

'Your father is fully aware of my financial position,' he cut in sharply, his voice icy now, 'which is one of the reasons why he approached me in the first place. I agreed to partner him in this venture at his insistence.'

'But the loss of the money doesn't mean anything to you,' she said furiously. 'Not really. How could you badger him—?'

'Dammit, girl, I haven't badgered him,' Carlton snapped tightly. 'If you remember, it was I who offered to help tonight, to try and find a way—'

'We don't need your help.' She saw Jennifer's hands flutter in protest with a soft exclamation of disagreement and turned on her sister like a small virago. 'And if you want your precious interview you have it, but not in this house. You don't care about Dad, not really. He could have died and you wouldn't even have been here. He could still die! What sort of world is this anyway where money is considered more important than a human being?'

She drew herself up and cast them all an icy look as she prepared to leave the room. 'We'll probably go under, Mr Reef,' she said at the door as she turned to hold his eyes across the room. 'But that needn't worry you at all, need

it? As you said when you phoned this house the day my
father had his heart attack, it was his ''stupidity and crass
ineptitude'' that caused it all anyway.' His harsh words had
been burning in her subconscious ever since they'd been
uttered and Carlton's face whitened as she flung them back
at him. 'But he's worth ten of you—of any of you.'

'Oh, really...' Jennifer's deriding voice wafted across the
room. 'I can't see what all the drama is about, for goodness'
sake. Anyone would think the old man was whiter than
snow when in fact he's been a right so-and-so most of his
life.' She stared at Katie scornfully. 'When has he ever been
there for you, then? Answer me that. I don't understand
you, Katie, I really don't. You're one of life's natural door-
mats.'

'No, I'm not.' Katie's face was as white as a sheet as
the enormity of the confrontation began to sink in. 'I love
Dad. I don't care what you think, Jennifer. You're incapable of love, and perhaps he is, but that doesn't make what
I feel for him any different, and he *has* been there for both
of us on lots of occasions in his own way.'

'Spare me the bleeding heart—' Jennifer's voice was cut
off as Carlton ground out her name through clenched teeth
before turning to Katie, his body tall and straight as he
stood up and his face calm.

'You're thinking with your heart and not your head,' he
said coldly as he walked across the room after picking up
his coat from the back of his chair. 'Probably the result of
the mental and physical exhaustion of the last few days.'

'No, it isn't.' He took her arm as she replied and led her
out of the room, shutting the door firmly behind the other
two. 'This is me; take it or leave it.'

'I'd prefer the former.' She had no warning as he enfolded her in his arms, his body hard as he held her close
to him, forcing her head back in a deep, long kiss that she
was powerless to resist, pinned as she was against his big

frame. Her brief struggles were ineffectual, only serving to move her more intimately against his body as he moulded her into him, his mouth devastating as it held hers.

And then, shockingly, she felt a response deep inside to the sensual lovemaking, a warmth in her lower stomach and a tightening ache in her breasts as they pressed against his hard chest that frightened her far more than his embrace. She had never, ever experienced such a reaction to male chemistry and was unprepared for the violence of the assault that came traitorously from within.

His tongue moved caressingly along her lips before invading the sweetness of her mouth and she felt her heart pounding with the thrill of it. She couldn't believe that a kiss could draw forth such blindingly shattering sensations as she was feeling now. Her head was spinning, her body was pure fluid as it melted into his and the rest of the world was a distant thing with no meaning or substance.

'Hell, you're lovely…' His voice was thick and deep and a sensuous, teasing tool in itself as his hands massaged her back, slipping under her thin cotton sweater with an ease that suggested he had done this sort of thing a million times before. 'I don't think you know the sort of power you have over a man…'

She wasn't aware that her arms had drifted up to his neck or that she was straining into him, searching for closer contact, as he took her mouth again. She was drugged, drugged with sensations that she had never dreamed existed but then, as his hands moved to her hips to draw her further against the hard evidence of his desire, cold reason returned in an icy deluge.

'Let me go.' It was a whisper but he heard it, freezing for a single moment before he put her from him without a word, striding down the hall and out of the front door without a backward glance.

CHAPTER THREE

KATIE leaned against the wall of the hall for long moments as she struggled to calm her spinning mind, hearing the roar of the Mercedes' engine as it left the drive far too fast and died away into the night.

How dared he? How dared he kiss her like that? she thought weakly as she forced her trembling legs to move and carry her towards the stairs. She reached the sanctuary of her room just as her legs gave way. He knew she loathed him; how could he take advantage of his superior strength so blatantly?

She scrubbed at her mouth with the back of her hand but the feel of his lips and body were imprinted on her flesh, going more than skin-deep. He was quite without morals, principles of any kind—that much was clear, she thought bitterly. But then who was she to talk after the wanton way in which she had responded?

She shook her head as she began to undress, walking through to the pretty *en-suite* bathroom in pale lemon and standing for long minutes under the shower as she let the warm water flow over her skin and hair.

After wrapping herself in a big fluffy bath-sheet she walked through to the bedroom again, looking round this room that had been hers since childhood, with its wonderful view over the half-acre of garden at the back of the house. Soon it wouldn't be theirs any longer.

She frowned as the enormity of it all began to seep into her consciousness. She had been concentrating so much on her father these last few days, so anxious that he wouldn't have another relapse, that she had pushed the financial disaster to the back of her mind in order to cope. But it was starkly in focus now and there was no escape from the knowledge of the effect that losing the family home would ultimately have on her father. He wouldn't be able to bear it. She thought back to the last few days before Carlton had given him a ray of hope and shook her head wearily. He had been waiting to die, willing it almost. And she'd sent Carlton away, insisting that they didn't need his help.

She groaned out loud, moving from the window to look into the full-length mirror-doors on her wall-to-wall wardrobes. Why had he kissed her? She inspected her face critically. She wasn't a beauty, whereas Jennifer was quite stunning. Large hazel eyes fringed with thick, dark lashes stared back at her, her wet hair clinging in curling tendrils to her shoulders.

She was averagely pretty, she thought with a little puzzled sigh, no more. Boyfriends had come and gone since she had started dating at sixteen, some more ardent than the rest, but none that had fired her with a grand passion.

She searched her face once more and then shrugged with a defeated sigh, quite missing the soft vulnerability in the hazel eyes and innocent appeal of her mouth that was more sensual to a discerning male than any flamboyant glamour. Maybe he had meant the kiss as a punishment for her harsh words? As she remembered all she had said her cheeks burnt with embarrassment. Oh, hell. She'd made a real mess of all this.

It was a long, sleepless night and she only drifted off into a heavy slumber as the birds began to sing in the old silver birch outside her window. She awoke with a terrible start a few hours later as Jennifer burst unannounced into her room, looking as fresh as a daisy.

'Come on, sleepyhead.' Her sister plumped herself down

on the edge of the bed and shook her without ceremony. 'I've sent Donald packing, so are we speaking again?'

'What time is it?' Katie struggled out of a disturbing dream that she couldn't recall and stared sleepily at her sister.

'Just gone nine,' Jennifer answered chirpily. 'Are you seeing Carlton today?'

'Carlton?' The name acted in much the same way as a bucket of cold water. 'I hardly think so after what I said to him last night.'

'You *were* a little emotional,' Jennifer said reprovingly, 'but perhaps he likes a bit of melodrama now and again. Anyway, it ought to be me who is mortally offended.'

'Why aren't you?' Katie asked shrewdly.

'Because you were only speaking the truth,' Jennifer answered disarmingly. Katie remembered this tactic of her sister's from the past—she always used it to devastating effect, especially when accompanied by the sheepish grin that, as she was doing now, melted the rather sharp features. It didn't mean anything but it *was* hard to resist, she thought wryly. 'Come on, Katie, I know I'm a pig but it's just the way I'm made,' Jennifer continued persuasively. 'Give me the gen on this Reef man, *please.*'

'There's not much to tell,' Katie said slowly, knowing she was being duped but beyond caring. 'Dad apparently approached him to go into this business deal with him and—'

'I don't mean *that*,' Jennifer interrupted caustically. 'What about his love life? Has he got a girlfriend? Is he keen on you? Any skeletons in the cupboard that you know of?'

'Jen!' Katie jerked upright in the bed as she brushed the hair out of eyes that were beginning to spark. 'Can't you forget you're a reporter for a few minutes?'

'Well, if I could, he's the man to make me,' Jennifer said

dreamily. 'You must have noticed what a dish he is, Katie. I know your sex drive isn't particularly frenzied but that physique coupled with those incredible eyes of his must have caused a few tremors, surely?'

As Katie opened her mouth to deny it she remembered the kiss of the night before and the way it had fired her body, and blushed scarlet, the protest dying on her lips.

'I thought so.' Jennifer narrowed her eyes at her sister, her expression thoughtful. 'But he has a certain reputation, little sister, in business and out of it, for going straight for the jugular. I wouldn't mess with him, sweetie; leave it to the experts.'

'Like you?' Katie slanted her eyebrows at Jennifer even as she had to laugh at her sister's outrageous manoeuvring.

'Exactly.' Jennifer stood up gracefully, stunning in white ski-pants teamed with a pure white cashmere sweater that would have cost Katie a month's salary. 'You never know, I might be able to...persuade him to do something to help us out.'

'You really do have the morals of an alley-cat, Jen,' Katie said lightly, half serious and half teasing.

'I know.' Jennifer seemed pleased at the comment. 'But life's so short, sweetie, and I do find sex such fun.' The feline eyes narrowed still further at the expression on Katie's face. 'Oh, hell, I've shocked you again,' she drawled lazily. 'When were two sisters ever such opposites as you and I?' She sauntered over to the window and pulled the curtains wide open, gazing down into the shining white world outside. 'I suppose you haven't met anyone since we spoke last?' she asked idly, without turning round.

'If you mean am I still a virgin why don't you just come straight out and ask?' Katie said tightly, well aware of the hidden question in her sister's apparently innocuous words.

'Oh, Katie, you're going to grow old and die here without ever having any fun if you're not careful.' Jennifer

yawned as she swung round and walked towards the door.
'What, or who, are you waiting for anyway? I haven't noticed many Prince Charmings beating a path to your door.'

'Jennifer, we're different; let's just leave it at that,' Katie
said firmly. 'You can go from man to man without it bothering you an iota; I just couldn't. And I do have fun, anyway. I go on dates when I feel like it and I've loads of
friends—'

'These are the 1990s, Katie.' Jennifer stopped at the door
with her hands on her hips as she frowned across at her
sister. 'People just don't go on dates without following
through.'

'Well, I do.' Katie was determined to end the conversation as soon as possible. 'And now I want to get dressed,
so if you don't mind vacating the premises...? And Dad is
waiting for a visit, don't forget.'

'I know, I know.'

'And later you are going to have to go through some of
the legal implications with me, Jennifer,' Katie added warn-
ingly.

'Oh, hell, darling, how tacky.' Jennifer wrinkled her nose
disapprovingly. 'Can't we just leave it to Dad and the solicitors?'

'Jennifer, when are you going to get it through your head
that he is an ill man?' Katie asked tightly. 'A very ill man.
He shouldn't be worried—'

'Well, you refused Carlton when he offered to help,' Jennifer snapped back abruptly, 'and frankly I think that that
was a hell of a moment to get on your high horse.' She
flounced out of the room before Katie could respond, bang-
ing the door in her wake.

Katie stared after her, her face dark with anger, before
she relaxed against the pillows with a deep sigh. Why did
five minutes with Jennifer always resemble several rounds
with Muhammad Ali? she asked herself silently, although

in this case she had to admit that that parting shot had been justified.

She shut her eyes tightly as she forced down the sick panic in her chest. She would have to ring him and ask if he would still help them, to eat humble pie... She pictured the scene in the hall in her mind's eye and shook her head helplessly. He was going to just love this. He must think he'd got them all exactly where he wanted them.

Perhaps she ought to leave him to Jennifer after all? she thought numbly even as something in her repudiated the thought of her sister in an intimate embrace with Carlton Reef. He was the sort of man who could well want a particular form of thanks for his assistance. She felt a little shiver of excitement flicker down her spine and despised herself for it. All this was sending her crazy.

The ringing of the phone downstairs interrupted her thoughts abruptly and a few moments later Mrs Jenkins popped her head round the door. 'Jennifer said you were awake,' she said cheerily as she placed a cup of tea on the bedside cabinet. 'And Mr Reef is on the phone—wants to speak to you and you alone.' The housekeeper's face twisted in a rueful grimace. 'That didn't go down well with your sister.'

'No, no, it wouldn't.' Katie's stomach had performed a violent cartwheel and she took a deep breath before lifting up the bedroom extension at her elbow. He was going to be mad, so mad. Was he going to make her crawl for help?

'Katie?' It was the deep, impatient voice she would have known anywhere and again that subtle little shiver trembled down her spine. 'Are you free this morning to go over those papers?'

'The papers?' She must sound like a complete idiot, she thought desperately as she struggled to compose herself. 'Oh, the papers. Yes, this morning would be fine.'

'I'll be over about eleven.' He hesitated for a split-second and she expected a few caustic words of admonition. 'And I'm taking you out to lunch. No argument, please; you need to relax a little.'

'Lunch?' Please help me to stop repeating the last word of every sentence, she prayed desperately. 'But the hospital—'

'Let Jennifer do a turn.' This time the dark voice held a definite bite. 'And you can call in this evening, can't you?'

'I…' It was an olive-branch and, in the circumstances, more than generous, she thought rapidly. She couldn't refuse. But to suggest that lunch with Carlton Reef could be *relaxing*? 'Thank you,' she said jerkily. 'Lunch would be lovely.'

'Good try, Katie.' The words were said with surface amusement but she sensed something underneath. 'For a polite acceptance, that is, but I'm well aware that you loathe the very ground I walk on. I'll see you at eleven and please have all the necessary correspondence ready.' And as the receiver was replaced at the other end she found herself still holding the phone, with her mouth wide open and her cheeks burning.

Jennifer managed still to be around when Carlton called at eleven, and was first to the door, almost pushing Mrs Jenkins over in her rush to get there. 'Hi there.' She smiled up at him as Katie appeared in the doorway of her father's study. 'Thought any more about that interview?'

'Couldn't think of anything else,' Carlton said mordantly as he raised a hand of acknowledgement to Katie, who was in the background.

'And?' Jennifer asked hopefully, pouting her lips beguilingly.

'It seems an even worse idea on reflection than it did last night.' Carlton's eyes were cool as he stared down at the lovely blonde. 'I've seen what papers like yours do to interviews, Jennifer.'

'Perhaps in the normal run of things,' Jennifer admitted reluctantly, 'but you know me, Carlton; you're a friend of the family. I wouldn't dream—'

'Jennifer, I don't know you from Adam,' Carlton said cynically as he moved inside the house, forcing Jennifer to back unwillingly to one side. 'And as for "a friend of the family"...?' He caught Katie's eye and the expression in his smoky grey eyes became positively derisive. 'Hardly.'

'But—'

'Now go and visit your father,' Carlton said drily as he walked towards the study without a backward glance. 'That *is* what you came down for, isn't it?' he added as he turned in the doorway and glanced at Jennifer's mutinous face. 'How long are you here for anyway?'

'Oh, whenever...' Jennifer murmured airily.

'Well, I'm sure we'll meet again.' Carlton smiled dismissively as he shut the study door very firmly and turned to Katie, watching her silently.

She stared back, acutely uncomfortable but determined that she wouldn't be the first to break the silence. Now that he was here, in the flesh, the sheer intimidating, sensual power of the man reached out to subdue and master her and the conciliatory feelings she had been experiencing all morning since his phone call took flight. She had never met anyone, her father included, who could challenge her with such absolute arrogance without uttering a word, she thought dazedly as the silence lengthened.

'Last night was not one of my better moves,' he said softly when the quietness reached screaming-point, 'but the only mitigation of what you would consider an act of gross boorishness was that it wasn't planned.'

It was the very last thing in the world that she had expected him to say and all coherent thought left her head as she stared dumbly back, quite unable to utter a sound.

'How mad are you?' he asked flatly, after a long moment.

'I—' She stopped abruptly as a feeling of utter bewilderment swept over her. She had flown at him, albeit vocally, in front of two other people and caused a scene, which was something she had never imagined herself doing in her wildest dreams. He had handled it with cool aplomb and amazing control in the circumstances, she reflected weakly, and even the kiss hadn't been unpleasant.

Far from it in fact, she thought silently as she turned and walked over to the desk where she had spread out all the relevant papers a few minutes before. He might have meant it as chastisement for her ill-chosen accusations, a lesson in discipline, but it had had quite a different effect on her nervous system.

'I'm not mad,' she said quietly after a long pause. 'I was way out of line, I know that. The important thing is that you're here now and prepared to try and help and I appreciate that.' She turned as she spoke and surprised an expression on the dark face that was gone an instant before she could catch it. Relief, hunger, a strange kind of vulnerability? But then he spoke, his voice cold and constrained, and the illusion was shattered.

'Good.' He joined her at the desk, careful to avoid the merest chance of any physical contact. 'Perhaps you wouldn't mind organising a cup of coffee while I glance through some of these?' He didn't look up as he spoke, his attention seemingly concentrated on the pieces of paper under his hands. 'And once I decide what's relevant we'll take them with us and photocopy them after lunch.'

'That's not necessary,' she said uncomfortably. 'If you just return them when you're done—'

'We'll photocopy them after lunch,' he repeated quietly as he raised his head and looked her hard in the face before resuming his perusal of the papers.

Jennifer was quite right, she reflected silently as she walked quickly from the room—those dark grey eyes of his *were* incredible. In fact, he was altogether too attractive for his own good and she had no doubt at all that he knew it. She could just imagine the women who must be after him and any man would get a swollen ego with all that he had going for him. Still...

She reached the kitchen and paused before she opened the door, her hazel eyes uncharacteristically hard. She had seen him in action that first day and knew what he was *really* like, and no amount of physical attraction could make her fall for a man who was the epitome of all the things she disliked most in a male. And she wasn't stupid. Even if Jennifer hadn't told her of his reputation she would have known his love life was busy. That one kiss had spoken volumes.

They left the house at twelve, stepping into a frosty, snow-covered world where the air was pure and bitingly cold and the sky a white-gold contrast against the bare black trees. 'Oh, how beautiful.' Katie stood for a moment on the top step and gazed across the drive. 'It doesn't seem real.'

'No, it doesn't.' His voice was thick and low and she turned as he spoke to see his eyes fixed on her face, their depths unreadable. He moved in the next instant, walking down to the car and opening her door as he continued the conversation. 'The roads are pretty hazardous, though,' he said expressionlessly.

'Are they?' That look had unnerved her but she fought for normality as she slid into the car, taking a deep, calming breath as he walked round the bonnet to join her. She had to remember last night as a warning and keep her distance mentally and physically from this man, she thought, because somehow, in spite of his cold authority and distant coolness, he had a fascinating aura about him that was frighteningly compelling. But it was just an illusion. She almost nodded to herself and caught the action just in time.

'So...' As he manoeuvred the powerful car out of the drive he glanced at her swiftly before concentrating on the road ahead. 'Tell me a little about yourself.'

'Me?' She shrugged deprecatingly. 'Not much to tell really. I'm twenty-three years old; I've worked as a teacher for the last two years.'

'Which school?' he asked quietly.

'Sandstone.' She didn't expect him to know it but there was a brief pause before he nodded slowly.

'The special school?'

'You know it?' she asked in surprise and he nodded again. 'My father wasn't too pleased when I took a job there,' she said tightly; the subject was still painful to her. 'He thought—'

She stopped abruptly and then continued quickly as she realised that Carlton would probably have felt exactly the same. 'He thought it showed a lamentable lack of ambition,' she said flatly. 'I had a good degree and he thought I should use it in other areas, like Jennifer. But I'd always wanted to work with children and the fact that this school was so close was an added advantage. It all seemed right.'

'Does it continue to seem right?' he asked expressionlessly, and she glanced at him quickly but could read nothing from the hard profile.

'Yes.' Her tone was both defensive and guarded.

'Then you clearly made the right decision,' he said coolly.

'I know.' She glanced at him again. 'I suppose you think like my father? That I should have gone on to do a Ph.D?'

'Then you suppose wrong.' He overtook a small family saloon before he spoke again. 'What sort of degree have you got anyway?'

'Joint maths and chemistry—a first,' she said quietly.

'I'm impressed.' He smiled slightly. 'But I'm more impressed that you followed your own star and did what you felt was right for you and I've no doubt at all that the kids in your charge feel exactly the same.'

He had taken the wind right out of her sails and she stared at him in consternation before transferring her gaze straight ahead. What was this? Some sort of trick, a game? He must be a fiercely ambitious man to have got to where he was so young. Had he really meant what he just said—?

'Why the frown?'

'What?' She jumped as the dark voice sounded in her ear.

'You're frowning as though I'd just said something out of order.' He swore softly as a large thrush suddenly flew out of the hedge bordering the narrow road and skimmed the bonnet of the car, missing it by a hair's breadth. 'Stupid bird's got a death wish.'

'Well, in spite of being on the outskirts of London this is still in the country,' she said quickly, glad of the change of conversation. 'My father—'

'You haven't answered my question.'

'What question?' she prevaricated weakly.

'Why were you frowning?' he persisted quietly but with an intentness that told her he wouldn't be deflected.

She thought about lying for a moment, passing the incident off with a light, amusing reply, and then found herself speaking exactly what she had thought. 'I can't believe a man like you would approve of my actions,' she said flatly.

'Why? Because your father didn't?' he asked softly.

'Partly.' She licked her lips which had suddenly gone dry. 'And also…you are very successful and ambitious; I would have thought you would have approved of my going on to do more important work.'

'You don't think handicapped children are important?'

he asked expressionlessly, his tone fooling her into thinking the conversation hadn't affected him.

'*I* do,' she answered hotly before she had time to think. 'I just didn't—' She stopped abruptly.

'You didn't think I did?' he finished for her. 'Charming. What exactly have you heard about me that you dislike me so strongly?' he asked grimly, his voice icy.

'Nothing,' she answered quickly, 'and I don't dislike you, not really. It's just that...'

'Just that?' he asked coldly.

'Just that your world is so different,' she said weakly. 'I didn't mean anything personal.'

'The hell you didn't.' He glanced at her once and she saw that the grey eyes were deadly. 'Well, in spite of what you may think, I consider your work very important, Katie, and I've just decided where we're going for lunch.' He had spoken as though the two things were synonymous and she stared at him, utterly bewildered, as he put his foot down on the accelerator, his face grim.

They drove for nearly half an hour in absolute silence and as the car ate up the miles she began to feel distinctly panicky. Where on earth was he taking her? she thought helplessly as the butterflies in her stomach began to do cartwheels. She glanced at him from under her eyelashes, intending to ask, and then bit her lip hard before she could form the words. She wouldn't give him the satisfaction but if he tried anything like last night again she would have the mental armour firmly in place.

She had seen her father in action too many times not to recognise that Carlton Reef was dangerous; men of their ilk regarded any show of compassion or tenderness as weakness and would capitalise on such vulnerability without the slightest stirring of conscience. It would seem that he was prepared to help her for the moment but she didn't doubt for a minute that he had reasons for doing so that she knew nothing about, or that he would be quite prepared to throw them to the wolves if it suited his purpose.

'We're here.' They were well into the heart of London now but in the last few minutes had turned off into a richly opulent area of the city where large, elegant detached houses stood impassively behind high walls surrounded by tree-filled grounds.

'Where's here?' she asked warily as he drove the car between two huge wrought-iron gates in a high stone wall and on to a small drive that finished in front of a particularly imposing residence in red brick.

'My house.' He cut the engine and settled back in his seat to survey her coldly through narrowed grey eyes.

'Your house?' she echoed in surprise. 'But I thought—' She stopped abruptly. 'Oh, are we photocopying the papers first, then?'

'Damn the papers.' He gave her one last long look before opening the door and walking round to the passenger side, his face grim. 'Come on.' He opened her door and offered her his hand.

'I don't think I want to come in,' she said warily as she glanced at his cold face. 'I'll just wait here.'

'You damn well won't.' He reached down and jerked her out of the car, his voice harsh. 'And frankly I couldn't care less what you want at the moment, Katie. I've never met a woman—' He stopped sharply. 'Like you,' he finished more quietly as he seemed to take hold of his temper.

She knew he had been going to say something more caustic and glanced at him once as he led her, still with his hand holding her arm, up to the wide semicircular area of concrete leading in a gradual slope to the front door. He bent down to insert the key in the lock and she noticed that the keyhole was exceptionally low but still the two things hadn't registered with any importance in her mind as the door swung open and they stepped into the hall.

'Carlton?' As the door directly facing them opened and a young man in a wheelchair appeared in the opening she froze. 'You're back sooner than I expected. Anything wrong?'

'Not at all,' Carlton responded easily as he drew her stiff body fully into the hall and shut the door quietly. 'I've just brought Katie home to meet you; anything wrong in that?' Her surprise was so great that she still couldn't formulate the right words in a mind that had suddenly gone blank. 'Katie, this is Joseph, my baby brother,' he added with a grin at the young man looking at them so interestedly. 'Joe, Katie.'

'Hi.' As the wheelchair scudded over to them Katie's wits returned in time with her heartbeat. 'Nice to meet you, Katie.'

'Likewise.' She smiled quite naturally, her eyes warm as she glanced down into a face that looked like a younger version of Carlton's but altogether more soft and gentle. 'Carlton didn't tell me he had a brother,' she added as she shook the hand held up to her.

'Then I'm way in front of you,' Joseph responded with a wry grin. 'I've heard quite a lot about a certain Katie White in the last week or so.'

'Have you?' Katie stared at him, her face expressing her incredulity as she tried to get her thoughts in order.

'I share all my business problems with Joe,' Carlton said smoothly as he took her arm again, leading her towards the room that Joseph had just left. 'And naturally the loss of a good deal of money was bound to come up.'

'Of course,' she answered quickly, missing the glance of warning that Carlton sent the younger man, who responded with a wicked grin and quick shrug of his broad shoulders.

'I'll go and organise some lunch.' Instead of following them into the room Joseph turned the wheelchair down the passageway to the left of the front door. 'I take it you *are* staying for lunch?' he asked Katie directly as she turned in the doorway to what was obviously the drawing-room.

'I don't know.' She glanced up at Carlton who was looking down at her, his face impassive. 'Are we?'

'If you'd like to,' he said quietly.

She looked at Joseph and nodded quickly, her warm smile in evidence again as her eyes met those of the younger man 'I'd love to, thanks.'

'Right, I'll let Maisie know.' He nodded at his brother cheerfully. 'And you can pour me a beer. By the way, I'm not going out again today.'

'I thought you were visiting that site in Kent later?' Carlton said.

'Under a foot of snow.' The wheelchair turned and fairly flew down the passageway as Joseph's voice trailed back. 'Meeting cancelled.'

'Joe's an architect,' Carlton said in explanation as he followed Katie into the room, shutting the door behind him before walking across to a well-stocked drinks cabinet in one corner. 'Doing very well for himself, too.'

'You should have told me.' He turned round at Katie's quiet voice, meeting her eyes as he gave a small shrug.

'Probably.' He eyed her expressionlessly.

'I could have said something wrong, offended him.'

'I knew you wouldn't,' he said simply.

'No, you didn't.' She flushed slightly but kept to her point. 'People can say all sorts of silly things when they're surprised.'

'And you were surprised, weren't you?' he said flatly as he flung his black leather jacket on to a chair. He was wearing a thick sweater teamed with black denim jeans and the result made her nerve-endings quiver as he walked over to stand just in front of her, lifting her chin with the tip of a finger as he looked down into the greeny brown of her eyes. 'In spite of knowing nothing about me there are a

whole host of preconceptions in there, aren't there?' He
tapped the side of her head gently as he turned away. 'What
would you like to drink?'

'Anything—white wine if you have it,' she said absently.
'Does Joe live here with you?'

'Uh-huh.' He passed her a glass of wine before speaking
again. 'The same accident that killed my parents left him
paralysed from the waist down at the age of thirteen,' he
said quietly, meeting the shock in her eyes with an expressionless face. 'I was abroad at the time, bumming around
Europe with a group of friends.' He waved to the big
leather sofa behind her. 'Have a seat.'

'Thank you.' She moved to a big easy-chair to one side
of the huge fireplace in which a log fire crackled and
sparked, holding out a hand to the blaze as she sat down,
as though she were cold. She wasn't, but the thought of
sharing a sofa with him was definitely out of the question.
'You're a little older than him, then?'

'Ten years.' If he had noticed the manoeuvre he didn't
comment on it. 'Joe's twenty-six.' So that made Carlton
thirty-six, she thought quickly as she nodded at him, taking
a long sip of wine as she did so. 'Once all the legal tech-
nicalities were sorted we bought this place and had it
adapted for Joe, although he spent a good deal of his time
in a special school in the early years.' The smoky grey eyes
held hers hard. 'Learning what he could and couldn't do
with people much like you, I suspect.'

'I'm sorry, Carlton.' She stared back at him as she nerved
herself to make the apology. 'What I said in the car would
have been right out of order whether there had been a Joe
or not. It was cruel and stupid.'

'Yes, it was.' He walked back to the sofa with his own
drink and sat down without taking his eyes off her face.
'The more so because I suspect you aren't usually like that.
What is it about me that hits such a nerve, Katie?' he asked

impassively. 'I don't think I've ever had anyone take such a violent dislike to me before and I'm curious to know why.' There was no emotion in his voice beyond faint interest but she was beginning to feel that he let very little of the real Carlton Reef show and wasn't fooled by the calm exterior.

'We just got off on the wrong foot, that's all,' she prevaricated quickly as she let her eyes drop from his. 'So Joe's an architect, then?' she continued, desperately searching for a change of conversation. 'He's done very well.'

'Four A levels and an excellent degree at Cambridge,' Carlton said quietly, unable to keep a note of pride out of his voice. 'He started a business with a friend of his when neither of them could get a job and it's going like a bomb now; he's hardly able to keep up with the amount of work. They're thinking of taking on a third colleague soon.'

'That's good.' She didn't know what to say. She had never felt so out of her depth in her life. The Carlton she had built up in her mind over the last few days, the harsh, uncaring, worldly philanderer, was metamorphosing in front of her eyes and she didn't like it; she didn't like it at all. It had been far easier to hate him when all was black and white; suddenly the amount of grey was more than a little disturbing.

But nothing has *really* changed, she told herself silently as she took another swallow of wine. He might be good to his brother but even the most selfish of men have the odd Achilles' heel; it doesn't mean anything in the overall run of things.

Suddenly the desire to leave, to get out of his presence and just run and run, was overwhelming and she bit her lip hard as she fought for control. No reason to panic, she told herself firmly; no reason at all.

The relief on her face was transparent a moment or so later when Joseph opened the door and wheeled himself in, and as she turned from smiling at him she caught Carlton's eye and saw that his face was icy. 'Steak and salad OK?' the younger man asked cheerfully as he took the beer Carlton held out to him. 'You've sent Maisie into something of a spin.'

'Maisie?' Katie asked him enquiringly.

'Our chief cook and bottle-washer,' Joseph said, with a wicked grin. 'We had a succession of live-in helps before Maisie turned up but Carlton was never satisfied with any of them. Mind you—' he turned from Katie and nodded at his brother's impassive face before grinning at her again '—when you see Maisie you'll understand why Carlton let this one stay.' He made an outline of the female figure with his hands. 'Real good to look at, eh, Carlton? As well as being the best little housekeeper this side of the Thames,' he added cheekily.

'Maisie is good at her job, that's all, Joe,' Carlton said with a slight bite to his voice. 'As you very well know. Now drink your beer and stop casting aspersions on the girl's character.'

Katie was surprised at how quickly the next half-hour sped by as she talked and laughed with Joseph, Carlton joining in the conversation once or twice but sitting slightly back from them as he surveyed them through cool, narrowed eyes.

She couldn't really take Joseph seriously—he was the original clown with a slightly childish sense of humour that nevertheless appealed—but he was exactly what she needed to relax. It amazed her that in spite of all he had gone through there wasn't a trace of bitterness or regret in anything he said, and in fact he seemed to have a confidence that was unshakeable coupled with an unswerving belief in his own fortitude.

She wondered how much of this positive mental attitude was down to Carlton and suspected that it was quite a lot.

There was no doubt that the two brothers were exceptionally close but then that was only to be expected in the circumstances, she told herself as she watched Carlton raise sardonic black eyebrows in silent amusement at something Joseph had just said.

When Maisie tapped on the drawing-room door to call them through to lunch Katie saw exactly what Joseph had meant as Carlton called her in to meet her. The girl was stunningly attractive, with huge liquid brown eyes and a long fall of sleek black hair almost to her waist. She smiled timidly at Katie and scuttled away after the briefest exchange of pleasantries, and Carlton smiled ruefully as they walked through to the dining-room just across the hall.

'She's very shy,' he said in a soft undertone as they followed Joseph, who was teasing Maisie about something as they entered the room, 'but she has one of the sweetest natures I've come across.'

Katie nodded and smiled even as a sudden dart of something gripped her heart. So he *was* attracted to the girl, she thought slowly as she sat down in the chair indicated. Well, it was only to be expected and absolutely nothing to do with her.

The room was exquisitely furnished in the same traditional style as the drawing-room, with heavy velvet drapes at the large full-length windows and expensive Persian carpets on the floor. This room was at the back of the house and the window overlooked a wide sweep of lawned garden, trimmed with large bushes and trees that had taken on a Christmas-card prettiness under their mantle of snow.

The meal went well, largely due to Joseph's irrepressible banter, and it was only as they were finishing coffee that Katie thought to check the time.

'It's nearly three o'clock.' She turned to Carlton in surprise. 'We ought to do that photocopying and then I must get back to the hospital.'

'How is your father?' Joseph asked quietly, his face completely serious for once.

'So-so.' She smiled but it was an effort. 'He's a very proud man and the thought of losing everything in the full glare of bankruptcy is hard for him to come to terms with.'

'It would be for anyone.' Joseph's eyes had darted to his brother as she had spoken but now centred on her face again. 'It's a wretched situation.'

'Yes, it is.' Carlton spoke dismissively as he stood up abruptly and indicated for her to do the same, resting his hands on the back of her chair and pulling it away from the table as she followed his lead. 'Let's go into my study and see to those papers.'

Joseph raised his eyes slightly as she followed Carlton out of the room and she smiled but said nothing, wondering what had caused the sudden departure but not caring to voice her confusion. Being around Carlton was like living on the edge of a volcano, she thought as she followed him down the hall and into a beautiful book-lined study at the far end of which a large coal fire was glowing bright red, giving the very male room a warm, comforting glow.

It had started to snow again outside, large feathery flakes falling thickly out of a laden grey sky, and Carlton stood looking out of the window for a few moments with his back to her before turning round suddenly and staring her straight in the face.

'Sit down.' It wasn't an invitation, more an order, and she did as she was told, sensing that something momentous was about to happen as she looked into his cold, grim face. 'It isn't much use photocopying those papers, Katie.' His voice was so devoid of expression that the portent of the words didn't sink in at first.

'It isn't?' She stared at him numbly.

'No.' He was still holding her eyes with a piercing gaze which she couldn't have broken if she had tried. 'I saw

immediately I looked at them today that there is no hope
of a reprieve. Your father signed several documents that
were...skilfully worded and in doing so lost any chance of
compensation. It was a forlorn hope at the best of times,'
he added quietly.

'I see.' Her face had whitened as he'd spoken, but other
than that she kept an iron grip on her emotions that wasn't
lost on the tall, dark man watching her so intently. The
brave tilt of her head, the dark anguish in the huge green-
brown eyes with their liquid appeal caused his mouth to
tighten into a hard line before he turned to look out into
the winter's afternoon again.

'You understand what I'm saying?' he asked tautly after
a few seconds had ticked by.

'Yes.' She stared at the broad back and wondered how
she was going to dash her father's hopes without breaking
down herself. It would have been better if Carlton hadn't
offered the little ray of hope, she thought desperately as she
remembered the painful appeal in David's face the last time
she had seen him. It would be almost as though he had lost
everything for the second time.

'But there is a way...' He turned and faced her again as
the grey eyes narrowed on her pale face. 'There is a way
we could turn things round.'

'"Turn things round"?' She rose jerkily from her seat—
she really couldn't sit still a moment longer—and walked
over to the fire, feeling as though she would never be warm
again. 'What do you mean, "turn things round"?' she
asked again, swinging to face him as his words sank
through the grey blanket that had descended on her mind.
'We're talking thousands and thousands of pounds' worth
of debts, aren't we?'

'Yes.' He was completely still as he watched her, an
almost menacing tenseness in his body that sent a fluttering
of chilling fear through her system as she looked into his

dark face. 'Several million if you take the house into account too.'

'Then how—?'

'I could pay the debts for you and give your father the house.'

'What?' The word came out as a breathless sigh but he seemed to hear it none the less.

'I could pay everything off,' he said again. 'You needn't even tell David the real circumstances if you don't want to.'

'But we could never pay you back.' She felt very strange as she spoke, the room and his big dark figure taking on an unreal quality that made the dream-like impossibility of his words even more insubstantial.

'Not in a financial sense, no.' He walked over to her as her heart began to thump frantically, an awful presentiment of what he might be trying to say freezing her mind and body. But he couldn't mean that, she told herself helplessly as he stopped in front of her. He didn't have to buy sex like any back-street voyeur in the less reputable parts of Soho; he could have any woman he wanted with just a raise of his eyebrows—and women far more beautiful and experienced than she was, at that.

'I don't understand,' she said weakly.

'I think you do.' He raised his hand slowly, as though in spite of himself, and touched the soft silk of her hair with one finger as his eyes moved slowly over her face. The sensual, expensive smell that seemed a part of him set her senses aflame as she stared up into his face, her eyes enormous. 'I want you, Katie. I want you very badly.' It was said without any emotion, a cold statement of fact that sent a shiver of fear flickering through her limbs.

'You're seriously saying you want to buy me?' she asked numbly, unable to take it in. 'That you want me to be your mistress?'

'Hell, *no*!' The explosion was immediate and she flinched at the anger on his face even as she knew a moment of profound relief that she had misunderstood him. Of course he couldn't have been saying that—she should have known. What would a man like him want with someone so naïve and ordinary as her, after all? She must have been crazy—

'I want to marry you, Katie.' Now she really *was* losing her mind, she thought as she stared at him in torpid insensibility. 'I want to marry you—a full marriage in every sense of the word with everything that that entails.' She knew her mouth had fallen open but there was nothing she could do about it. 'After which every debt would be cleared, every last penny paid off, the whole slate wiped clean.'

He stood back a pace and eyed her sardonically as his eyes registered her horrified shock. 'So it's really over to you,' he said slowly as he crossed his arms over his muscled chest and narrowed his eyes like a great black beast waiting to pounce. 'The grand sacrifice or disaster; a way of escape or a long walk down the painful road of financial ruin that you've been trying to save your father from so desperately.

'Decision time, little Katie White; decision time.'

CHAPTER FOUR

'You can't be serious.' Katie stared up at him helplessly. 'I mean...' Her voice trailed away as she found herself utterly lost for words, her face portraying her horror at the suggestion.

'On the contrary.' His brief smile was quite without humour and didn't touch his eyes at all.

'But why on earth would you want to marry *me*?' she asked weakly. 'You must know loads of women who would be only too pleased to jump at such an offer.'

'Must I?' He considered her quietly through narrowed eyes. 'Perhaps that's the problem.'

'I don't understand.'

'Then let me explain it to you.' He indicated the chair that she had vacated with a wave of his hand and as she sat down he turned to look out of the window with his back to her and his dark face hidden from her gaze. 'I'm a wealthy man, Katie, a very wealthy man, and that in itself brings a certain set of...difficulties. As you just pointed out, a certain type of woman who is looking for an easy ride for life would appreciate a tailor-made meal ticket to keep her in the style to which she is accustomed.' The deep voice dripped sarcasm. 'I want children but I want something more than a clothes-horse as their mother, you understand?'

'No.' As he turned to face her she shook her head slowly. 'I don't. Surely you must have met someone you liked, someone who would be suitable—'

'You're suitable.' The piercing grey eyes were unreadable. 'You are beautiful, spirited, and your attitude to life

75

and values are in line with what I would look for in the
mother of my son.'

'Your son?' This was getting out of hand, she thought
desperately. 'Look, I really don't think—'

'Joe will never be able to have children,' Carlton continued quietly as though she hadn't spoken. 'The succession
of the Reef name is down to me and I do not intend to
leave my estate to a cats' home.' He eyed her consider-
ingly. 'I am thirty-six years of age and I feel the time is
right to settle down and produce a family but as yet I
haven't met a female I would consider suitable—or I hadn't
until you came on the horizon. Besides which—' He
stopped as she twisted restlessly.

'But we don't even like each other.' She spoke quickly
before she lost her nerve, still unable to believe that he was
really serious. 'You can't possibly think a marriage between us would work? It's... Well, it's—'

'The only way out of your problems,' he finished coldly,
the dark veil that had settled over his face as she had spoken masking his thoughts. 'Unless of course you would
prefer to see your father lose everything he has worked for
all his life? The decision has to be yours.'

'But we don't even *like* each other,' she said again, her
voice urgent. 'And I don't want to marry anyone.'

'I do not dislike you, Katie.' Just for a moment something dark and fierce burst in the depths of the grey eyes
and then a shutter banked down the fire and his face was
ruthlessly implacable. 'And, like I said, I want you. You
cannot deny that there's a certain physical chemistry between us?'

'I—' She stopped abruptly. How could she explain to an
experienced man of the world like him that she had thought
every woman reacted the way she had to his maleness, that
her response to him would have been something he would
have expected, nothing out of the ordinary?

'If the physical side of a marriage is OK everything else will fall into place,' he continued smoothly, 'and with us it would be, I can assure you.'

'How can you know?' she asked weakly. 'You don't—'

As he pulled her up and into his arms she was too dazed by recent events to resist, although her body tensed, expecting a fierce, overwhelming assault on her senses. But his kiss was delicate, meltingly, deliciously delicate, as he traced the outline of her mouth and her closed eyelids with soft, butterfly kisses that were achingly sweet.

And then his mouth found the hollow of her throat where a pulse was beating frantically and she heard her little moan of desire with a throb of embarrassment even as she tilted her head further, allowing him greater access.

This was crazy... But the thought couldn't compete with what his mouth and body were doing to hers. Sensation after sensation washed across her closed eyes as a trembling warmth shivered through her limbs. He was good at this, oh, he was very, very good, she thought helplessly as his fingers explored the length of her spine in a sensuous, warm caress that made her aware of every inch of her body, her breasts heavy and full as they pressed against his hard chest and her lower stomach achingly hot.

'So perfect...' As his mouth took hers in a deeper, penetrating kiss he moved her more firmly into his body, his arousal hard and dominant against the softness of her hips, leaving her in no doubt as to what she was doing to him. 'Now do you doubt it?' He moved her slightly from him as he spoke to look down into her face, his eyes glittering. 'We would be good together, Katie, I know it.'

She came back to reality with a hard jolt as she opened her eyes to stare into the dark, triumphant face in front of her. All this had been a cold-blooded exercise in proving a point? But of course, what else? And she had fallen into his arms like a ripe plum? Self-disgust was bitter on her tongue as she adjusted her clothes with shaking hands, her cheeks burning.

'Do you doubt it?' he asked again, his voice almost expressionless now as she glared at him before turning away, mortally embarrassed.

'I don't know.' She shook her head blindly as she walked over to the fire, holding out her hands to the warm blaze as she kept her face in profile to him. 'I've never—'

She stopped abruptly and then forced herself to go on. He had to know, after all. He'd probably assumed that she had slept with other boyfriends, that she was at least a little experienced. 'I'm not used to the physical side of a relationship,' she managed stiffly, her face hotter than the fire now. 'I've nothing to judge by.'

There was utter silence in the room for several moments and then he spoke again, his voice quiet and low. 'Does that mean what I think it means?'

'Yes.' She wanted to curl up and die with embarrassment but the need to justify her statement was paramount. 'And not because I haven't had offers,' she said tightly. 'I just haven't happened to meet anyone I liked enough, that's all, and for the last few years my job hasn't left me much time for socialising.'

'You don't have to apologise—'

'I'm not!' She interrupted his quiet voice sharply as she turned to face him, expecting mockery, contempt, even derision, but the hard face was completely expressionless—curiously so. 'I'm not,' she reiterated more quietly. 'But you're used to more experienced women. I wouldn't be able to...' Her voice trailed off as she found herself completely unable to finish what she wanted to say.

'I get the message.' His voice was very dry. 'You think I'm looking for a cross between a performing chimpanzee and a modern-day Jezebel between the sheets, is that it?'

'Well, aren't you?' His cool composure was the last

straw. 'From what I've heard—' She stopped abruptly, aware that she had been about to be less than tactful.

' ''From what you've heard''?' he repeated softly—so softly that she was fooled into thinking that he was unconcerned until she looked into his eyes. 'And what exactly have you heard, Katie?' he asked grimly, his voice quiet and even. 'And who from?'

'It isn't important.' She shrugged with a lightness she was far from feeling.

'The hell it isn't.' He moved the two steps to the fireplace in a moment, his face tight with controlled rage. 'Someone has been filling your mind with stories and I would like to know who.'

'It isn't like that.' She raised her gaze to his as she spoke, her hazel eyes jade-green in the dim light. 'And you have no right to question me like this, no right at all,' she added quietly as she forced herself to stand her ground and not flinch away from his rage. 'You're a millionaire and people are bound to be interested in your private life. It's human nature.'

'Jennifer...' He breathed the name between clenched teeth as he looked down into her face. 'Of course, I might have known.'

'I didn't say—'

'You didn't have to.' He nodded grimly. 'And you believed every word which came from such a reliable source?' he asked cuttingly, his voice icy and his narrowed eyes tight on her face.

'Look, this is ridiculous.' She sat down in the chair as her legs began to tremble, taking a deep breath as she did so and forcing her voice to remain calm. 'It doesn't matter one way or the other, does it? I can't marry you; you must know that. We barely know each other and, anyway, the whole thing is...immoral.'

' ''Immoral''?' he repeated savagely. She watched him

take an almost visible hold on his emotions as he glared down at her, his eyes glittering hotly, and when he next spoke his voice was cool and controlled, only his eyes betraying his inner fury. 'Hardly, Katie,' he said softly. 'People marry for much less reason than we have, I do assure you. There are still countries where arranged marriages are the normal procedure and the rate of success is very high, much higher than in the Western world where so-called ''love'' dominates the game.'

'You don't think it's right to marry for love?' she asked quietly, appalled by his cynicism.

'I didn't say that.' Something flickered in the back of his eyes and was gone. 'But love is a transient thing, all too often here today and gone tomorrow. If you married me I can assure you that I would never look at another woman and I would expect absolute fidelity from you in return. I can make you that promise in the cold light of day without any messy emotion gilding my words. You would gain immediate solvency for yourself and your father and my protection both physically and financially for you and yours for the rest of your life.'

'You really *are* serious,' she whispered slowly. She moistened suddenly dry lips with the tip of her tongue and as his eyes followed the gesture, a dark heat flaring briefly in their grey depths, she felt her stomach tighten in response to his desire. The full enormity of what marriage would mean, in all its intimacy, flooded her senses and she shut her eyes for a moment as its rawness overwhelmed her.

'Oh, I'm serious, Katie.' Her eyes snapped open to meet his cool, sardonic gaze and their eyes held for a full ten seconds before she broke the spell, lowering her head quickly as she took a shuddering breath. 'I've never been more so,' he added.

How could he be so cool, so unemotional about it? she asked herself weakly in the few seconds before she raised her head again. He was treating the whole thing almost like a business deal, a clinical merger. Even her father had more emotion than this man. And however he dressed the proposal up he was buying her as a breeding machine for his offspring. No more, no less.

She steeled herself to look at him calmly and keep her voice steady. 'I'm sorry, Carlton, but I can't accept your offer, generous though it is,' she said stiffly. 'And I'm sure you will be able to find someone far more suitable for the perpetuating of the Reef name.'

Her father would understand, he *would*, she told herself desperately as she met the cool grey gaze that was carefully blank. He wouldn't expect her to make such a sacrifice...would he? 'I really think I'd better go now,' she added uncomfortably when he still didn't speak. 'I'd like to visit Dad tonight.'

'Of course.' She could read nothing that indicated his feelings in either his face or voice; they could have been discussing the weather a few minutes previously instead of the joining together of their bodies and future in matrimony. 'Would you like me to drop you at the hospital or at the house?' he asked quietly as he walked across the room and opened the door, his body relaxed and controlled.

'The house, please.' She smiled nervously, but as he opened the door and stood for her to pass through the grey gaze didn't centre on her face. 'I want to pick up my car.'

The drive home was the sort of unmitigated nightmare Katie wouldn't have wished on her worst enemy and the tense, electric atmosphere in the car wasn't helped by her growing panic at the thought of what she had refused. They had been given a way out, something she had imagined impossible just days earlier, and she had thrown it away without even considering it.

She sneaked a quick glance at Carlton's harsh, dark profile from under her eyelashes and her stomach churned

painfully. But she'd had no choice. To marry him, to actually *marry* him? She couldn't.

She glanced at his large, capable hands on the steering-
wheel, the dark body-hairs disappearing into his sleeves,
and again that little thrill of something hot and alien shivered down her spine. What would it be like to be made
love to by such a man?

She caught the thought firmly and locked it away before
it could develop. She would never know. She didn't *want*
to know. But even as she chastised herself the elusive smell
of his aftershave was doing crazy things to her hormones.

'Goodbye, Katie.' He had left the car, intending to open
her door, but she was too quick for him, almost falling out
of the luxurious interior in her eagerness to escape before
he could touch her. He paused to lean against the bonnet
as she backed away towards the steps, his face cool and
sardonic and his eyes veiled. 'The offer still stands, you
know.' His voice was cold and formal. 'I'd prefer you to
think about it for a day or so before you make a definite
decision. It would be advantageous to both of us.'

'I—'

He interrupted her by dint of raising one very autocratic
hand. 'Goodbye, Katie.' The dismissal was very definite.

She watched him slide back into the Mercedes as she
stood at the bottom of the steps and although the air was
already redolent with the tang of frost she still stood there
long after the car had vanished, her mind whirling in a
maelstrom of fear and excitement and confusion. Just a few
days ago she had never heard of Carlton Reef. Her normal,
safe little world had been ticking on in the same old way,
no big highs and no lows.

She turned to look up at the house, mellow and lovingly
familiar in the dusky light of the dying day. And now this
could go, along with everything she had always thought of
as theirs. She shook her head slowly. And she still wasn't

convinced her father was going to get well. She put her
hands up to her head, feeling as though it would burst with
the force of her thoughts.

'No more thinking.' Her breath was a white cloud in the
bitingly cold air as she spoke out loud into the silent, snow-
covered evening. 'Just one step at a time.'

Her father was alone, dozing in an armchair next to his
bed, when she reached the hospital half an hour later. She
had been unable to see Jennifer's car in the car park but as
it had been almost full she hadn't paid too much attention.

'Katie?' David White opened tired eyes as she sat down
quietly next to him. The sight of him rent her heart. For
the first time that she could remember he looked every inch
his age, his big, broad-shouldered body strangely vulnerable in the old, thin hospital blanket that someone had
tucked round his waist, and his head bowed, as though the
effort to hold it upright was too much.

'Hi, Dad.' As she bent to kiss him she prepared herself,
subconsciously, for the usual turning away of his head, but
tonight it didn't happen. Instead she found her kiss accepted, welcomed even as his mouth met hers, and the
shock robbed her of conversation as she leant back in her
own chair. 'How are you feeling?'

'How do you think I'm feeling?' The irritable, exasperated voice was the same, however. 'These damn nurses are
forever fussing in and out; it's like Piccadilly Circus in here
most of the time. How they expect anyone to get better in
this place is beyond me—you need an iron constitution just
to survive.'

'Well, you'll be fine, then.' She smiled at him as he
glared his irritation. 'Did Jennifer come in to see you?'

He indicated a bowl of grapes on the top of the hospital
locker with magnificent disgust. 'She stayed long enough
to give me those and then went off in a huff because I told

her what to do with 'em,' he said testily. 'If she had to bring anything at all a half-bottle of Scotch would have gone down well.'

Katie closed her eyes for a moment and prayed for patience. 'And you needn't look like that,' he continued flatly. 'You know as well as I do that the only reason she came was out of duty and because you'd badgered her to make the effort.'

'Dad—'

'I know Jennifer, lass.' The pale blue eyes were cynical now. 'And there's no need to make any excuses for her. Unfortunately she inherited most of me and very little of her mother, unlike you.' She stared at him in surprise, her mouth falling open in a little O. 'And she's astute enough to know I read her like a book,' he added quietly. 'Jennifer will always do unto others before they do unto her, whereas you…' His voice faded as he shook his grey head slowly. 'You worry me to death.'

'I worry you?' For a moment she thought she was hearing things. 'Why do I worry you?'

'No matter.' He waved his hand at her, clearly embarrassed, his voice gruff and his face scowling. 'How did you get on with Carlton? Did he find anything of interest?'

'Well…' She hesitated, unsure of how much to say.

'I feel in my bones there is a solution, Katie.' It pained her to see the eagerness in his face, the light of hope in the tired blue eyes. 'And if there is one Carlton is the man to find it. He's one of the hardest men I've ever come across but he's fair. Oh, yes, he's fair,' he added almost to himself, nodding with his thoughts. 'He'll find a way out.'

How was she going to tell him? She bit her lip as her stomach turned over. It would have to be now. He would know sooner or later anyway and it would be better hearing it from her than from someone else.

'I was born in that house, you know, lass.' He raised his

eyes to hers again and she was shocked to see the suspicion of tears in their watery brightness. 'Your grandparents were never around much, always partying here and there or away out of the country, but although I didn't have any brothers or sisters I was content with my nanny, living quietly at home. That house sort of became father and mother to me, I suppose.

'Your mother understood that; yes...' he nodded again '...she understood. And first Jennifer and then you were born under its roof.'

'And here was I thinking you weren't sentimental,' she teased softly, taking refuge in lightness as the ache in her chest threatened to spill out in tears, and when a knock at the door sounded a second later, followed by the entrance of two of her father's old cronies, she had never been more pleased to see anyone.

She sat with the three men for a few minutes before leaving, promising her father that she would call in the next afternoon, and walked out to the car park feeling as though she had just received a death sentence.

She knew what she had to do; she had known it all along, really, from the moment Carlton had made his amazing offer. If her father lost everything, if he was stripped of even his pride and dignity along with the house, he would give up and die. She knew it. And Carlton knew it too.

She remembered his face in the study and clenched her hands together in tight fists as she took big gulps of the icy cold air. He was attracted to her physically, he wanted a certain type of wife quickly, and she fitted the bill. And he was prepared to pay an exorbitant amount of money for the privilege.

She walked slowly to her car, her head spinning. Money was no object to him; he could probably buy and sell them ten times over without even noticing. But it was all so cold-blooded.

She sat in the driving seat without starting the engine, her mind numb and desperate. Cold-blooded and inevitable. Could she go through with it? She sat for a moment more before starting the engine suddenly, her face white but her mouth determined. Of course she could. There was no other choice. She would face this as she had faced all the other twists and turns of life over the last thirteen years and draw on her own strength and determination to get her through.

But Carlton Reef? She pushed the sudden panic and fear aside with a ruthlessness her father would have been proud of. He was a man, just a man, whatever her fanciful mind tried to make of him. This feeling that he was different in some way, that he could affect her as no other man ever could or would, was merely the result of long, sleepless nights worrying about her father and their financial catastrophe, of trying to find a way out of the maze of problems and difficulties that formed a living nightmare whether she was asleep or awake.

And now she had a solution. She negotiated the car out of the hospital gates as her stomach turned over. And she would take it without flinching, with no more hesitation, because lifelines such as this were only thrown once, and if the dark waters of despair and misery closed over her father's head because she had let her fingers slip on the rope she would never forgive herself.

CHAPTER FIVE

'CARLTON?' She had rung him as soon as she'd got home.
There was no point in delaying the decision and she didn't
want him to visit her father and tell him the truth. 'It's
me—Katie.'

'Katie?' The deep voice held a note of concern. 'Is anything wrong? Your father is all right?'

'I've changed my mind.' There was a blank silence at
the other end of the phone and, after waiting a moment,
she plunged on, her voice trembling and her nerves quivering with a sudden fear that it was too late, that he'd already regretted what was, after all, an amazingly generous
offer. 'If you still want to marry me, like you said this
afternoon, then—' She took a deep breath and prayed her
voice wouldn't betray the thick panic that was consuming
her. 'Then I agree.'

She waited with bated breath for his reaction and
couldn't have explained even to herself what she wanted it
to be. Just hearing his voice sent shivers down her spine.

'Why?'

'Why?' she repeated. His voice had been strange, thick
and husky, and now she felt a sick dread that he *had*
thought again, and had realised that he was giving far too
much and receiving very little in return. He could have
almost any woman he wanted; it had been madness to think
he was for real. She should have known—

'Why have you changed your mind?' he asked in his
usual voice now, the tone slightly wry and definitely cool.
'I presume you've been to visit your father tonight?' he
added quietly, as though the two things were linked.

'I've just got back.' There was no point in lying. If this crazy idea was going to get off the ground, and it didn't seem too promising at the moment, then at the very least she was going to have to be completely honest about everything. 'He wasn't too good,' she continued painfully, 'and I don't want... I don't want him to lose this house,' she said slowly. 'It means far more to him than you could realise, more than even I knew. I'm frightened he won't get better if he has to see it go,' she added when he still didn't say anything, her voice very small. 'In fact I'm sure he won't.'

'I see.' There was a brief pause. 'Did you say anything to him?' he asked quietly, his voice devoid of any expression.

'No.' She took a deep breath as her heart began to thud so hard that it actually hurt. 'He had other people there.'

'So he doesn't know yet? Are you going to tell him about...our arrangement?' he asked flatly.

'No.' The answer was immediate and instinctive. 'That would make everything just as bad. He has to think that you've found something, done something that enables him to keep the house through his own good fortune. We'll have to tell him that we—we've fallen in love,' she added painfully.

'And you think you can fool him?' Carlton's voice was gentle and for some reason that very fact made her knees tremble. 'You think you can act that well?'

'We'll have to.' She closed her eyes tight and prayed for calm.

'I didn't say ''we'',' he said slowly. 'I can do my part, but can you do yours?' There was a strong element of doubt in the deep voice.

'Of course.' She still wasn't sure if he was saying yes or no. 'I can do anything at all if it helps him to get well.'

'I'm not so sure, Katie.' There was a moment's silence.

'Unlike nearly every other woman I know, you would not make a good liar.' There was a note in the deep voice she couldn't identify and she would have given anything to see his face at that moment. 'You know I want you and I'll agree to anything you want regarding David but he is not a fool. He's a very astute and intelligent man, and, more than that, he loves you. That makes him particularly perceptive where you're concerned.'

'Carlton, just because I'm his daughter, it doesn't automatically mean he loves me,' she said with a flat pain that wasn't lost on the man listening to her. 'You don't understand—' She stopped abruptly. There was no way she could tell him how the years had been since her mother had died. She couldn't tell anyone—it was too complicated, too harrowing to put into words. 'Things aren't always black and white,' she continued slowly.

'No, I know that,' he said blandly.

'It has to be as I've said.' She paused, searching for a way to make him understand. 'If he thought he'd been bailed out, that in some way he had still failed and lost the house through his own misjudgement, he wouldn't try again,' she finished painfully.

'And he's not trying now, is he?' Carlton said gently. 'You've noticed that too. He's in danger of giving up.'

'Then you agree?' she asked carefully, her nerves jumping wildly.

'Yes.' The answer was immediate. 'I told you, I want you, Katie. I want you very badly.' There was that thickness in his voice again that sent a little shiver flickering down her spine. 'And you're aware of exactly what you're promising?' he asked slowly.

'Of course.' She couldn't keep the note of indignation out of her voice. She was twenty-three years of age, for goodness' sake, and after several years at university she was well aware of the facts of life, in all their diverse branches, even if she hadn't actually participated herself.

She remembered the paper-thin walls of her small room on campus and the energetic activities of one of her friends next door, whose morals had matched Jennifer's, and smiled mentally. Carlton would be amazed at what she knew! There had been mornings when she had found it difficult to face Sally without blushing!

'Shall I come round now?' he asked quietly.

'*What*?' For a heart-stopping moment she thought he was demanding his proposed marital rights immediately, and from the note of unforgivable amusement in his voice when he next spoke she knew he had recognised her blunder.

'Relax, Katie...' His voice was soft and deep and she shut her eyes against its seductiveness. 'I was merely asking if you would like me to come round to iron out the details tonight.'

'No.' She took a deep breath and prayed for dignity. 'The morning will do.' The morning will more than do, she thought weakly.

'I'll see you at eleven.'

As the phone went dead she blinked in surprise, standing with the receiver in her hand for a good half-minute before she replaced it slowly and glanced about the wide, spacious hall.

Everything looked the same. The beautiful wood panelling still gleamed and shone in the dim light, the expensive water-colours in their gilt frames, which her mother had loved so much, still hung silently in place, and yet everything was irrevocably, frighteningly different. She had just promised to marry a man she didn't love and who didn't love her. A marriage of convenience.

She heard Jennifer's car draw up outside and then the sound of her sister's key in the lock at the same time as

Mrs Jenkins appeared from the kitchen at the end of the hall.

Well—she squared her shoulders as she prepared to tell them her news—this was where the acting began and it had better be the performance of her life. If she couldn't convince them she would never convince her father and too much depended on her for her to fail.

Carlton arrived dead on eleven the next morning and, inevitably, it was Jennifer who got to the door first, opening it with a dramatic flourish and smiling up at him with as much charm as she could muster, considering she was green with envy.

'Have I got the scoop of the year or what?' She slanted her eyes at him with more than a faint touch of malice in their light blue depths. 'I take it I can print the news Katie told me last night?' she added smilingly. 'Especially as you are going to be my brother-in-law.'

'I thought you'd be pleased.' Carlton's voice was very dry.

'Oh, I am, I am.' She watched him carefully, her eyes speculative. 'Mind you, I think you're marrying the wrong sister.'

'Is that so?' He smiled down at the slightly feline face in front of him, recognising the social repartee and a little amused by it, but as he opened his mouth to say more Katie walked down the stairs, and when Jennifer saw the look in his eyes as he gazed at her sister she accepted defeat.

'My, my, my, so it's really true...' she drawled softly as Katie reached the bottom of the stairs, and as Carlton sent her a swift glance from narrowed eyes she smiled again, her face even more cat-like. 'Wedding-bells and orange blossom even? I have to admit I did wonder if anything untoward was going on last night when Katie told me you were going to get married.'

'Once the reporter, always the reporter, Jennifer?' Carlton asked as Katie joined them. 'Sorry to disappoint your fertile imagination but this is just a case of good old-fashioned romance, isn't it, sweetheart?' As he bent to take Katie's lips in a swift but possessive kiss she didn't have to act the immediate response her body made to the intoxicating smell and feel of him.

'Love at first sight?' Jennifer asked softly, her eyes tight on Carlton's face as he drew Katie to his side, his arm round her waist. 'Just like all the best stories?' she added cynically.

'For me, most certainly.' He smiled lazily as he held Jennifer's gaze. 'Katie took a few days longer but I convinced her she couldn't live without me in the end.'

'Lucky old Katie.' Jennifer smiled sweetly but the pale blue eyes remained as hard as glass. 'Who would have guessed? It looks like Dad's little bit of misfortune was destiny, after all.'

'And that's not as bad as it could have been.' Katie entered the conversation for the first time, treading warily. Her sister was too cute by half and the years of being a reporter had honed her natural sense of shrewd cunning to rapier-sharpness. It was clear that she was suspicious of this whirlwind romance, although Carlton's easy, assured handling of the affair this morning had mellowed the edge of hard scepticism in the slanted blue eyes.

'Storm in a teacup,' Carlton agreed smoothly. 'Now, if you'll excuse us, Jennifer, I've got a few things to discuss with my new fiancée.'

'Oh, don't mind me.' Jennifer looked distinctly put out as Carlton turned from her with a dry smile. 'I'm just part of the furniture.'

'I'm taking you out to lunch.' As the dark grey eyes rested fully on her face Katie felt her senses leap helplessly.

'Can we leave now?' he asked softly, his voice warm on her overwrought nerves.

'I'll get my coat.' Anything to escape Jennifer's hawk-like stare! she thought hurriedly.

As they drove away Katie was aware of Jennifer's face at the window and raised a hand in farewell which was ignored. 'Your sister doesn't approve of me?' Carlton had noticed the little by-play with some amusement, a cynical smile curving the hard sensual mouth.

'Oh, she approves of *you* all right,' Katie answered candidly. 'It's me she doesn't think much of. She thinks she'd make a far better Mrs Reef than I.'

'And what do you think?' he asked her softly.

'I think she's right,' Katie answered honestly, after a moment of hesitation. Well, he had asked, and that was exactly what she did think, after all.

'That devastating honesty.' He glanced at her briefly and she saw that although his mouth was smiling his eyes were cold. 'I shall have to remember only to ask you questions I might like the answers to. I don't know how much of this my ego can take.'

'I didn't mean—' She stopped abruptly. 'Well, you know women find you attractive, don't you?' she said uncomfortably. 'And Jennifer—'

'What about you?' he interrupted her coolly at the same time as he pulled off the main road on to the verge and cut the engine almost in one movement. 'How do *you* find me?'

She stared at him warily. She hadn't seen him in this mood before. The cold, ruthless, austere Carlton Reef of the business world was gone but in his place was someone... Someone she wasn't sure how to react to. His eyes were still veiled, giving very little away, his face cool and slightly mocking, but there was something... She swallowed silently as fire trickled down to her nerve-endings.

'Katie—' He stopped as though searching for the right

words as she gazed at him. 'We're entering into this thing for our own reasons; you know mine and I know yours.'

He paused and glanced away out of the window, his eyes remote. 'And I'm aware that I'm not your ideal man, so don't worry that I shall expect any protestations of undying love, either now or in the future.' The dark eyes swung back to her for a second but she couldn't read anything in their cool greyness. 'But if I've misread the signals, if you don't find me even physically attractive...well, human sacrifices were never my scene.' He eyed her as her cheeks burnt scarlet.

What on earth did he expect her to say? She could feel her face growing hotter and hotter. 'I do.' When the ensuing silence got too much to bear she forced the words out. 'Find you physically attractive, that is.' Too much for comfort, she added silently.

'Well, that's a start.' He raised her chin with one finger so that her eyes met his. 'Isn't it?' he asked softly.

'Yes.' She was amazed and horrified at what the light contact of his skin against hers was doing to her and even more so at the dizzy confusion his words had produced. She *knew* he was marrying her simply because he had decided, in a cold, logical, emotionless way, that it was time for him to have children, and she fitted the requirements he had laid down for his future wife. He wanted her physically, and he had bought her when the opportunity had arisen. She wanted to close her eyes against the knowledge but it was there, hot and vibrant, in her soul.

So it was imperative that she keep her own space, that she didn't let any little part of the real her become vulnerable or exposed. He didn't love her; he had never pretended that there was any chance of that now or in the future; he had been totally honest.

But she wasn't a man. And now she did shut her eyes for a fleeting moment. She didn't have his cool, logical, predatory approach to life and love, and already she wasn't sure how she was beginning to feel about him. It wasn't just his looks, impressive though they were—it was *him*. There was a magnetism, a fascinating aura about the man that was dangerously compelling and although she knew it would be sheer emotional suicide to fall for him—

'Katie?' He interrupted her racing thoughts by reaching into his pocket and extracting a small, and obviously old, dark velvet box. 'I'd like you to wear this.'

'What is it?' She lifted the tiny lid carefully and then stared astounded at the exquisite antique ring that the box held. 'Carlton...' Her eyes shot to his face. 'It's the most beautiful ring I've ever seen.'

'It was my mother's, and her mother's before her.' He took the ring out of its snug setting and reached for her left hand. 'May I?' There was a thickness in his voice, a husky warmth that turned her insides to melted jelly, and as she obediently held out her hand he slipped the ring on to her third finger and held her eyes with his own before leaning forward and drawing her into his arms.

His mouth was caressing, arousing, bringing an immediate hot, aching response from her that frightened her half to death. What was this power he seemed to have over her? she asked herself, panic-stricken, but as his hands moved over the small of her back, warm and knowledgeable, she ceased to think and just let herself feel.

The kiss was hot and sweet and full of a subtle awareness of her own needs that made it devastatingly irresistible. Not that she wanted to resist. She had never felt like this before, never known it was possible to feel like this.

As his lips moved to the pure line of her throat she felt herself shudder, but she was helpless under his caress, no more able to hide her response to his lovemaking than fly.

There was passionate heat in his mouth now as he bit sensuously at her lower lip before plundering the sweetness of her inner mouth. His hands moved from her back to cup her breasts through the soft wool of her sweater, his thumbs stroking their tips, which hardened and swelled at his touch, and when she heard the soft moan that hung trembling in the air for an instant she didn't realise for a full ten seconds that it was her voice.

And then he moved away, settling back in his own seat almost lazily as she struggled to come to terms with how he could make her feel with seemingly very little effort.

'I thought we'd drop in at the hospital on our way to lunch.'

'What?' She gazed at him for a moment as though he were talking in a foreign language and then forced herself to respond normally as she pulled her coat around her, the engagement ring heavy and alien on her hand. 'Oh, yes, fine,' she agreed dully.

'It can only hasten David's recovery to know every-thing's under control,' Carlton said evenly, his voice cool and contained, and for a moment she could have hit him for his impassive countenance. How dared he sit there so cool and relaxed when she was a shivering wreck? she asked herself angrily. And everything was far from being under control. Light-years away in fact. 'Do you feel up to it?'

'Up to it?' She felt a flood of pride and burning humil-iation at his quiet words. He thought his lovemaking was so wonderful that she would collapse at his feet, did he? That it would render her incapable of talking to her father? 'Of course I feel up to it,' she said with an icy coolness that made his eyes narrow. 'I'd rather get it over and done with as soon as possible. I've never lied to my father about anything before.'

'And now you've got to convince him that you're madly in love with a guy you don't even like,' Carlton drawled mockingly, his eyes tight on her profile as she smoothed her hair into place with the help of the small make-up mirror in her bag. If she had been looking at him she would have seen a tenseness to his mouth that belied the easy voice, but she wasn't, and his tone fired her temper still more.

'Exactly.' She turned her head to look out of her side-window, allowing the silky fall of her honey-blonde hair to shield her face from his gaze. 'But needs must.' He might have women falling at his feet from every direction but she was blowed if she was going to add to their number, she thought silently.

'Quite.' He started the engine without another word and as they drove in absolute silence along the icy roads, heaped on either side with banks of snow that the snow-ploughs had cleared, she stared blindly out of the window at the white world outside until her gaze was drawn to the ring again.

It *was* beautiful, she thought miserably. Exquisitely so. The centre was a large diamond that flashed with breath-taking majesty over a circle of tiny rubies and pearls that surrounded it and in between each stone the gold was worked in lacy folds that enhanced the clearness of the jewels. And it had been his mother's, and his grand-mother's... Perhaps she shouldn't have accepted it in the circumstances, she thought suddenly. An ordinary ring, just a token, would have done.

'Carlton...' She didn't know quite how to put it but she had better say something. 'This ring.'

'Yes?' His tone wasn't exactly forthcoming but she glanced at the hard profile and took a deep breath.

'If you would prefer to keep it I wouldn't mind. I'd quite happy with something less expensive, even a dress-ring if you'd rather—'

As the car slammed off the road and on to the verge for the second time in ten minutes her stomach turned at the look on his face. He was angry, furiously angry, but what had she said?

'Let's get one thing absolutely clear here and now, Katie,' he said tightly, each word punched into the air with such force that she shrank from them. 'This is going to be a real marriage and as my wife you will be expected to wear the Reef ring. There will also be much more expected of you, not least from me, I might add.' He glared at her angrily. 'When I make a deal I stick to it and I expect those I'm dealing with to do the same.'

'I know that.' After the first moment of shocked surprise she had straightened proudly, her eyes flashing.

'Good.' He glared at her a moment longer and then ran a hand through his hair in a gesture of utter exasperation. 'Oh, hell, I don't want to frighten you—'

'You don't,' she lied promptly, two spots of colour burning in an otherwise pale face. 'I just wondered if you'd felt that you had to offer me your mother's ring, that's all—if you felt obliged—'

'Katie...' Her name was a sigh, but in the next instant his voice held that mocking, caustic note that she had heard before. 'No, I don't feel I "have" to do anything,' he said slowly as he flicked the ignition again. 'When you get to know me better you'll understand I never do anything I don't want to.'

They arrived at the hospital without having spoken another word and Katie felt her stomach churn at the prospect ahead as Carlton parked the big car and cut the engine. He took her arm as they entered the building and she forced herself not to flinch from his touch although her nerves reacted violently to his closeness as he drew her into his side.

'A smile might help,' he said softly as they came to the door of her father's room. 'If you can't quite manage the dewy-eyed bride approach.'

She flashed him a glance of pure venom and then stitched a smile into place as he opened the door, his mouth twisted with cynical amusement.

She was amazed at how well things went—mainly due, she had to admit, to Carlton's easy mastery of the situation. David was delighted, transparently so, at their news, although there was one nasty moment when Carlton left them alone at the end of the visit.

'Katie?' Her father took her hand in his, the first time she could ever remember him voluntarily touching her. 'This is all very sudden, isn't it?'

'Dad, we're two grown adults, not a couple of teenagers,' she replied carefully. 'There's no need to wait if we're sure, is there?' She looked into the eyes of this man whom she had always loved but had remained steadfastly remote from her since the death of his wife, and forced a smile from somewhere. She hadn't really expected him to question her; she hadn't thought he would care that much.

'And you are? Sure, I mean?' he asked urgently, his pale blue eyes searching her face. 'Don't get me wrong—I like Carlton. In fact he's one of the few men I like as well as respect. When he makes a commitment to anything or anyone it's made and that's rare these days, but...' He paused, his face thoughtful. 'You're young and your heart rules your head. You aren't doing this out of some sort of misguided gratitude because Carlton helped us find a loophole, are you?'

She forced an easy laugh from somewhere even as it registered that he was still holding her hand tight and that the soft light in his eyes was something he hadn't allowed her to see in a long, long time. 'As if I would...'

'Oh, you would, Katie White, you would,' her father said quietly. 'I know you, lass. You're too like your mother in the things that matter. I was always glad I'd met her almost before she was out of pigtails so that I could protect her from herself,' he added with a flat, hard pain that caught at her heartstrings.

'Were you?' Something of her utter amazement must have shown in her face because he shook his head slowly, shutting his eyes as he lay back against the pillows and letting go of her hand as his face flushed a dull red with hot embarrassment.

'I'm tired, Katie.' It was the normal sort of brush-off she had received over the last thirteen years if she ever tried to break through his hard outer shell, but it still hurt. She stared at his lined face for a long moment before rising from her chair and placing a careful kiss on the side of his cheek.

'OK, Dad.' The years of training kept her pain from showing in her voice. 'I'll call in later.'

'No need.' He opened his eyes, his face straight and his eyes veiled now, the softness gone. 'Jennifer is coming this afternoon, so I understand, and no doubt there'll be other visitors. Enjoy the day with Carlton.' The withdrawal was complete.

She smiled but said nothing and left quietly to join Carlton who was waiting in the corridor outside. 'OK?' His eyes were piercing on her face. 'No problems?'

'Not really.' But her mouth was tremulous and the dark grey eyes missed nothing.

'He didn't buy it?' Carlton asked quietly.

'Yes, yes, he did.' They began to walk towards the lift some yards away and she lowered her head in the gesture he was beginning to recognise.

'Katie?' Just before they left the warmth of the centrally heated building he took her arm, turning her to face him, his eyes searching her face. 'He cares very much for you, you know. He just finds it hard to express it.'

'Does he?' She wasn't going to crumble, she told herself tightly as the unexpected sympathy constricted her chest.

'You don't know him like I do, Carlton; you don't under-stand.'

'Perhaps you know him too well. Sometimes an outsider can see things more clearly,' he said with a gentleness that made her instinctively gather her defences before she crum-bled in front of him.

'Sometimes,' she agreed bitterly, forcing the weakness aside.

'But not in this case?' he asked carefully.

'Definitely not in this case.' She shook off his arm wea-rily and opened the door to the blast of arctic air outside. 'But he likes you, Carlton; he likes you very much indeed,' she said quitely as they walked towards the car. 'You're very like him, you see; he understands you.'

'And that's another black mark against me.' Her eyes snapped up to his face then but she could read nothing from his expression to indicate how he had meant the cool state-ment.

'No, of course not—'

'You don't lie well, Katie, like I said before, so just stick with the big whopper for now,' he said grimly. 'I'm aware that you disapprove of me and I don't altogether blame you so let's leave it at that for now. Is there anywhere in par-ticular you'd like to eat?' he asked abruptly as he opened the car door for her.

'I—n-no...' The change of conversation had her stam-mering like a schoolgirl, she thought with a sudden burst of anger that banished the ache in her heart over her father. Why did this man always reduce her to a quivering wreck anyway? It just wasn't fair. She wanted to be cool and calm and in control.

They lunched at an olde-worlde pub that was all horse brasses and copper warming pans but the food was sur-prisingly good and Carlton proved to be an entertaining companion when he set his mind to it, with a sharp, slightly cruel wit that had her laughing more than once, even though she slightly resented the fact without understanding why. But she did understand that he was dangerous, she thought to herself as she watched him return with their drinks, after they had walked through to the bar from the charming little dining-room. Dangerously attractive, dangerously male, *dangerous*. And she was going to marry him.

'Have you a date in mind?'

'What?' It was almost as though he had read her mind, she thought faintly as he sat down beside her at the little carved wooden table, depositing her dry white wine in front of her with an easy smile.

'For the wedding.' The black eyebrows rose fractionally. 'And do you want all the trimmings? A white dress, bridemaids and so on?' he asked with indulgent easiness.

'I haven't really thought about it,' she prevaricated quickly, mortified at the touch of colour she could feel in her cheeks.

'Then think.' He was still smiling but there was a touch of steel about his mouth now. 'I thought the beginning of June would be suitable. That will give you a few weeks to fuss about your dress and all the other details and we could have a month's honeymoon at my villa in Northern Spain and get to know each other.' She blushed bright red now at the immediate picture in her mind, but if he noticed he didn't comment on it. 'Later we could perhaps take a cruise, spend the winter abroad if you would like that?'

'I—' She was floundering again and hated herself for it, but the careless ease with which he spoke of their future plans left her breathless. 'I don't mind. Whatever you think.'

'Submissive as well as beautiful?' The dark voice was both amused and mocking and grated on her nerves like barbed wire. What did it matter what she thought anyway?

she asked herself painfully as she averted her eyes from his. She was nothing to him beyond a body in which to nurture his precious heirs; he had made that perfectly clear, and she would have to come to terms with that.

But somehow... Somehow, the more she got to know him, the harder that became. She wanted him to see *her*. The self-knowledge was frightening, opening her as it did to a vulnerability that she was sure he would capitalise on if he sensed it.

But he couldn't read her mind. The thought enabled her to raise her head and smile with a composure she was far from feeling. 'But of course.' She took a sip of her drink and carefully placed the glass back on the table, pleased to see that the trembling inside was hidden and that her hand was perfectly steady. 'You are paying a great deal for me, Carlton. It's only fair that I give value for money.'

As his mouth straightened into a thin line and his eyes took on the consistency of splintered glass she realised that she had gone too far, but there was no way she could take the words back. They had been a defence, a desperate cover for her bruised feelings, but she hadn't liked their ugliness and she suspected that Carlton liked them still less. But it was too late now. There was nothing she could do but brazen it out.

'Is that how you really see things?' he asked coldly after several seconds had ticked by in deathly silence.

'What other way is there?' she asked dully.

'Dammit, Katie!' The explosion was sudden and frightening but even as she shrank back from him and the heads of the only other couple in the bar turned their way the perfect control was back in place, the only betrayal of the rage burning inside in the glittering darkness of his narrowed eyes as they fixed on her white face.

'You're making this harder than it needs to be,' he said

quietly. 'You do see that? If you give yourself half a chance you might even find you like me.'

That's what terrifies me, she thought painfully. She had gone through the whole gamut of emotion since the first moment she had heard his voice on the day her father collapsed, but none had been as frightening as the one that was creeping insidiously through her veins now.

She *knew* he was like her father—cold and austere and devoid of normal human warmth. She *knew* that he was ruthless, that he had had lots of women—hadn't Jennifer confirmed that very thing? He would find it easy to mould her to his will, to pick her up and drop her whenever he felt like it. She had seen her father do it time and time again with different females since her mother's death. She knew all that. It was a solid weight in her chest that was there night and day.

So why, knowing it, did she still have the urge to reach out and touch his face and ask if they could begin again as though the last few days had never happened? To beg him to look at her, really look at her, and see her for what she was rather than the future mother of his children?

She had spent thirteen years trying to win her father's love and approval; she couldn't spend the rest of her life trying to win Carlton Reef's, and for that reason she had to keep herself detached, remote from this thing that was going to happen to her. It would be hard, but the alternative was unthinkable.

CHAPTER SIX

THE next few days rushed by at breakneck speed, for which Katie was thankful. It gave her less chance to think and that way she could function on automatic. She explained to the headmaster at the school that it would be necessary for her to leave after Easter, and although he was reluctant to see her go he was more than understanding about the position she was in.

'We shall miss you, Katie, but I didn't think we'd hang on to you this long,' he said warmly as she sat across the desk from him in his small office. 'And you know that there's always a place for you here.' The brown eyes smiled with real friendliness.

'Thank you.' His kindness had touched her. 'And I'll always be available to help out now and again once I'm married if anyone is sick. I'll let the office have my new address and telephone number.'

'That'd be useful but we know you've got a lot on your plate, what with your father and all.' Mr Mitchell patted her arm as she rose to leave. 'But if you wouldn't mind doing the odd bit of supply teaching in the future it would be a great back-up for us. Your fiancé wouldn't mind?'

'No, no, of course not.' Would Carlton object? she thought as she left the orderly little room and walked back to the general staffroom. She had no idea. She stopped still in the corridor as the full enormity of it all swept over her again. She didn't know him, what he thought, how he would behave as a husband...

She pushed the whirling thoughts back into the box she had kept them in for the last few days and closed the lid

105

firmly. She wouldn't think about it now. All that would have to wait. Just getting through each day was enough for the moment, what with the host of arrangements and plans to discuss each night and with her father expected home at the end of the week.

Carlton insisted on coming with her to fetch David the following Friday evening and she was glad of his hard male strength as they wheeled him to the Mercedes outside the main hospital doors. 'Damn fuss!' David White was red with anger at the ignominious position he had been forced into. 'There's nothing wrong with my legs.'

'It's not your legs we're worried about,' Carlton said mildly as he opened the passenger door and helped him into the car. 'And stop acting like such an idiot, David. You've had a couple of major heart attacks in as many days and you either knuckle down to good advice or you break your daughter's heart. Which is it to be?'

Grey eyes met pale blue ones and neither was prepared to give an inch. As Katie watched them she felt a bubble of laughter for the first time in days. It looked as if her father had met his match at last. The thought sobered her instantly.

Once he was home, Mrs Jenkins fussed around him, patently ignoring his bark and avoiding his bite, helping to establish him in his study, which she and Katie had converted to a bedsit over the last few days. Katie sat on the end of his bed while he ate a light supper.

'You do see it's better for you to avoid the stairs for the time being?' she asked him warily as Carlton walked in with a bottle of Scotch that made David's eyes light up. 'And this room is huge, and it looks on to the garden, and the cloakroom and loo are right next door—'

'All right, all right, all right…' He raised a hand in protest. 'I give in—for the moment,' he added quickly.

'And you promise you'll take your pills and rest?' She

thought she might as well press the point while she had Carlton for back-up. 'It's important, Dad.'

'He knows that.' Carlton had poured two hefty measures of whisky into two tumblers as she had been speaking and handed one across to him with a wry smile. 'He might be a cantankerous old so-and-so but he's not stupid.'

'Well, thank you.' David's voice dripped sarcasm. 'I was beginning to wonder if everyone thought my brain was addled as well as my body.' But he accepted the whisky with a nod as Carlton sat down on an easy-chair by the side of the bed and stretched out his long legs.

'Should you have that?' Katie asked anxiously but as both men gave her a withering glance she acknowledged defeat, took her father's tray from the bed and left them to it.

Much later, after a short phone call to Jennifer, who was back in her flat in London and preparing to dash off the next day to the wilds of Scotland on some story or other, and after checking the guest list for the wedding, Katie was sitting finishing the wedding invitations when Carlton walked into the drawing-room. 'He's asleep.'

Ignoring the tightening in her body that his presence always induced, she lifted what she hoped was a calm face and smiled carefully, but it was hard not to betray what his big body, clothed casually in jeans and a black sweatshirt, did to her nerve-endings. 'Thank you for staying with him tonight, Carlton.'

'No problem.' He shrugged as he flung himself down in a chair opposite the large sofa, where she was sitting with the invitations spread around her. 'I thought he needed some sort of normality after all those days in hospital so we chatted about business and so on.' His eyes were fixed on her face. 'He's totally accepted our explanation, by the way, even congratulated me again on acquiring you for my future bride. He hoped I realised that I was the luckiest man this side of heaven.' Her eyes shot to his face and Carlton smiled easily.

'Did he say that?' she asked with a painful casualness that wasn't lost on him.

He nodded slowly. 'That he did,' he said softly. 'Do you want to know how I replied?'

The room had become still, very still, and she found she was holding her breath as she looked into the dark, handsome face opposite her. 'I—' But then she jumped violently at the shrill intrusion of the telephone ringing loudly at her side and lifted the receiver to the sound of Carlton's muttered curse in the background. 'Yes.'

'Katie, is that you?' It was Joseph's voice. 'Is Carlton still with you? There's some emergency or other with his American office.'

'Just a minute.' As she handed the telephone to Carlton she rose quickly, scattering invitations over the floor. 'Would you like a coffee?' she asked quickly.

'Fine,' he nodded before speaking into the receiver and she left the room quickly as though the devil himself were on her heels. There had been something in his face during those last few seconds, something dangerously hypnotising. Was that how he looked at his other women before he made love to them?

She found that she was clenching her hands tightly against her side and forced herself to relax them slowly, finger by finger. But he'd said that once married to her he would be faithful. Did she believe that? She toyed with the question as she busied herself fixing the coffee. She really didn't know. What if he fell in love with someone else? The thought caused her heart to jump violently. What would he do then?

'Why such a deep frown?' She nearly jumped out of her skin as his voice sounded just behind her, and turned to see him leaning in the doorway, his hands thrust into his jeans pockets and his dark eyes glittering as they wandered over the soft gold of her hair.

'Carlton, what if—?' She stopped abruptly. She had almost been going to say "you". 'What if either of us falls in love with someone else?' she asked quickly, before she lost her nerve. 'What happens then?'

He straightened, anger darkening his eyes and stiffening his body as he moved to stand in front of her. 'Is this a rhetorical question or is there something you're trying to tell me?' he asked softly as he lifted her chin to look into the soft greeny brown of her eyes, his mouth hard.

'No, I'm not trying to say anything,' she protested quickly. He smelt good; he smelt so, so good. 'I just wondered—'

'Quit wondering.' As his mouth came down hard on hers she realised that there was more than a touch of anger in the kiss—almost a fierceness that bruised and punished, but it didn't seem to make any difference to her traitorous body, which leapt into immediate and vibrant life.

In fact, the only time she was alive, fully and completely alive, was around him, she realised helplessly as he ravaged her mouth with a raw desire that was shockingly pleasurable. His hands firm in the small of her back, he moulded her into the length of him and shaped her against his arousal so that the embrace was almost like an act of physical possession.

It should have shocked her, she knew that, but, instead of anger or self-disgust at her wanton response to his aggressive domination, she gloried in it, gloried in the fact that she could make him want her so badly.

When he released her they were both breathing heavily, and as she touched a finger to her swollen lips his eyes followed the gesture, self-contempt turning his eyes black. 'I'm sorry, Katie; I didn't mean to hurt you,' he said thickly as he turned and walked to the doorway.

'Carlton?' Her voice stopped him as he was about to leave. 'I didn't mean—I haven't met anyone.'

He turned to face her and nodded slowly, his face expressionless now and his eyes veiled. 'Good.' His eyes stroked over her face, flushed and warm, and over the tousled silk of her hair. 'Because I don't share what's mine, Katie, not now, not ever. And I would kill anyone who tried.' She stared at him, her eyes wide. 'Does that answer your question? And skip the coffee; it's getting late. I'll see you tomorrow.'

Once Easter had come and gone and she no longer had to work each day, Katie found that she was dividing her time between her own house and Carlton's most of the time. His limitless wealth had smoothed the arrangements for the wedding like magic in spite of the comparative haste.

The church was booked and she had chosen her dress— a fairy-tale concoction of ivory silk and old lace over a wide hooped skirt and tiny fitted bodice. The staff of the madly expensive hotel where Carlton had booked the reception for over two hundred guests had fallen over themselves in an ingratiating desire to satisfy his every wish, and even Jennifer's dress—her sister was her only bridesmaid—was hanging ready and waiting in her wardrobe at home.

The fact that all that side of things was taken care of had left Katie free to organise some changes at Carlton's home—a suggestion that had come from the man himself.

Since that night when David had come home Carlton had maintained a cool, almost distant approach to her when they were alone that Katie didn't understand. In company he was the perfect fiancé—charming, attentive and always ready to please—but when they were alone... Katie wrinkled her brow as she smoothed the last fold out of the new curtains in the room that was to be their bedroom. He was reserved, wary even. Always holding himself in check.

'Hi.' She turned to see Joseph in the doorway. Carlton had had a chair-lift installed in the early days of Joseph's accident so that he was able to move about the house freely. 'Maisie says lunch will be ready in twenty minutes.'

'Lovely.' She smiled warmly at Joseph. The more she had seen of Carlton's brother, the more she liked him, and the two had found that an easy, friendly relationship had developed between them almost without their realising it.

Maisie she found harder to communicate with. The girl was an excellent housekeeper but painfully shy and the only person she really seemed to open up to was Carlton, a fact which Katie had to admit, in the odd moment of self-analysis, she didn't like. And the way he was with Maisie— gentle, protective even… She brushed the thought aside as Joseph wheeled his chair into the room.

'What does Carlton think to all this, then?' he asked cheerfully as he glanced round the room that had been Carlton's. He had been sleeping in one of the spare bedrooms while she redecorated this one. 'Does the master approve?' he asked cheekily.

'Uh-huh.' She smiled down at the face that was so like her fiancé's, and waved her hand expansively at the dusky grey curtains and carpet, and deep scarlet duvet that covered the large four-poster bed. 'It was a compromise.'

'Bodes well for the future.' She nodded but the shadow that passed over her face wasn't lost on him. 'Anything wrong, Katie?' he asked casually as he wheeled his chair across to the large full-length window and looked out into the garden, lit with soft May sunshine.

'Not really, it's just that—' She hesitated, unsure of how much to say. Although she and Joseph got on well he was still Carlton's brother and fiercely loyal. She didn't want him to think that she was criticising Carlton behind his back. 'He's a very private person, isn't he?' she murmured quietly. 'It's hard to know what he's thinking.'

'Persevere.' There was a note in Joseph's voice that made her join him at the window and as she sat on the carpet at his side he looked down at her, his face open and direct. 'The last thirteen years or so haven't been easy for him, Katie, looking after this house, the business, being father and mother to me.' He hesitated, then continued slowly and quietly as though he found his thoughts difficult to express.

'I went through a bad patch after the accident. I was just a kid, Mum and Dad were gone and I couldn't bear to think I'd never walk again, that I was a cripple for life.' The last few words were full of pain and she put out a hand to him, her eyes soft. 'At the time I took all the care and love Carlton gave me as my right; kids can be very selfish...' He paused, his expression reflective.

'Carlton dedicated himself to me in those early days, gave me the will to fight, to go on, and I slowly came to terms with it all. It was a long time later that I realised just what he'd had to sacrifice too.

'He'd been involved with a girl, Penny, at the time of the accident. They'd been going to get married. Oh, it wasn't official—' he flapped a hand '—nothing like that but he'd told me and they'd started to make plans.

'Well, like I said, he put in a lot of time with me in the early days and Penny began to object. A helpless little kid brother wasn't her idea of the best start in the world to married life. She made his life hell for a time, trying to make him choose between what she saw as a millstone round his neck and herself, and then one day he found her in bed with someone else and that was that.'

He eyed her warily and she forced herself to keep her face blank and betray none of the pain that had hit her like a ton of bricks. 'It hit him hard—he's the original still waters that run deep—but he'd never talk about it after he told me what had happened. But from that point—' He paused abruptly. 'Well, he played the field, I guess. You know that.'

'Yes.' It hurt. It hurt far, far more than she would have thought possible and everything in her wanted to ask him if he thought Carlton still loved his first love, but she couldn't. She was too frightened of what the answer might be.

'And then he met you.' Joseph looked up at her as she rose slowly to her feet. 'And I could see straight away you were the real thing.'

'Could you?' For a moment she almost told him—told him that this whole thing was a sham and that Carlton was merely acting a part, but she bit back the words before they passed her lips.

'Sure.' He grinned as she forced a smile to her face. 'The way he looks at you, his voice when he speaks your name—I never thought to see him like this but, like I said, still waters run deep. But it's difficult for him to open up, Katie; he's always been like that, but more so after Penny. Don't give up on him.'

She nodded blindly. Well, she'd brought this on herself; she should never have started the conversation in the first place. But oh—she found she was gritting her teeth as she followed Joseph out of the room to go downstairs for lunch—why couldn't she have affected him the way this Penny had?

The thought shocked her and she immediately tried to explain it away. Of course it would be better if he had some feeling for her—they were going to be married for good-ness' sake. That was all she wanted, just some sort of nor-mal human warmth. She didn't love him and she knew he didn't love her but they were going to commit a good part

of their lives to each other. It was only natural that she
wanted some solid basis to build on, wasn't it?

She continued to talk to herself all the way downstairs
and into the kitchen where the three of them ate at lunch-
time at the huge wooden kitchen table that Maisie kept
scrubbed snow-white.

Maisie glanced up as they entered, her beautiful velvety
brown eyes lowering swiftly as she quickly began to place
the cold meat, jacket potatoes and salad on to the table. For
the hundredth time since she had first come into this house
Katie found herself wondering about the relationship between Carlton and his housekeeper.

She couldn't fault Maisie. The girl was sweet and quiet
and almost painfully timid and yet there was something…
Something in those big brown eyes that she couldn't quite
fathom. And Carlton was…different with her. Whereas
Joseph would tease and chaff Maisie he always managed
to keep her at a distance too, but Carlton… He was defensive, protective even.

The thoughts that had been forming for weeks solidified.
She wasn't imagining it, she *wasn't*. But she couldn't ask
him about it. Her wedding was only three weeks away and
yet she couldn't really talk to the man she was marrying.
The urge to scream and shout at the tangle she had made
of her life was overwhelmingly fierce but she bit it back
painfully.

By the time she arrived home later that afternoon the
tension had culminated in a pounding headache at the back
of her eyes. Carlton was taking her out to dinner that night
and she had never felt less like seeing him. There was such
a mixture of emotions swirling about in her head that she
couldn't identify just one and yet she knew that if he cancelled the evening she would be unbearably disappointed.

'You look tired.' Her father raised his head as she
glanced into his room where he was sitting reading a book.

He was much better although he still tired easily and the fact that he hadn't insisted on returning to his old room upstairs before now told Katie that he was aware of his weakness. 'Doing too much, no doubt, just like your mother.'

He had taken to mentioning his wife more and more in the last few weeks and Katie loved it. The fact that she could talk about her mother with him, for the first time since she had died, was beginning to ease the ache in her heart that always accompanied thoughts of the woman she had loved so much.

'I'm OK.' She walked over and bent to kiss him and he raised his face to meet hers. It had happened several times now but it always stunned her. He had changed and mellowed since his illness, she thought. He wouldn't thank her for saying so but it was true. She sat a while with him, discussing her day and making something out of nothing to entertain him, and then wandered upstairs to shower and change.

At eight, when she heard Carlton's voice downstairs after an imperious ring of the doorbell, she was ready to join him. After the snow and blizzards of March May had entered as gently as a lamb and the night was warm and soft, the scent of summer hanging heavy in the air. He had warned her that he would be taking her to a nightclub so she had dressed accordingly in a chic sleeveless cocktail dress in midnight-blue with a short silky jacket that she had spent hours finding a few days before. It had cost the earth, but the expert cut of the material and the much needed confidence the dress gave her was worth every penny, and now she stared at her reflection in the mirror anxiously.

She'd left her hair loose to wave in soft tendrils about her shoulders, and had used just a smudge of eyeshadow to enhance her eyes, which now stared back at her, wide and speckled with light beneath fine, arched brows. She wished she looked older. She frowned at the artless reflection irritably. Older and sophisticated and more... More cosmopolitan.

She grimaced at her thoughts, snatched up her bag from the chair and left the room quickly, running down the stairs on light feet.

'Hi.' It had only been twenty-four hours since she had seen Carlton last but as she entered her father's room and he turned towards her, drawing her into him with a casual arm round her waist and kissing her lightly—for her father's benefit, no doubt, she thought testily—her senses went haywire. Her response to him only intensified the feeling of vulnerability, of unworldliness she had felt in the bedroom and she didn't like it but...there was absolutely nothing she could do about it either.

'Hello.' She moved away from him as soon as he released her in the pretence of folding back the covers on her father's bed. 'You won't be late to bed, Dad?'

'Fuss, fuss, fuss.' David fixed her with hard, gimlet eyes, clearly annoyed at being treated like a child, and Carlton surveyed her through narrowed grey slits that told her he had recognised her manoeuvre and didn't like it. She stared back at them both as an unfamiliar recklessness snaked through her veins. Just at this moment in time—and she knew it wouldn't last—she didn't care about what either of them thought.

'Well?' She smiled with dazzling brightness at them both before settling her gaze on Carlton's dark face. 'Shall we go?'

'Of course.' She saw the narrowed glance he gave her as they walked through the hall and realised, with a little thrill of gratification, that for once he wasn't quite sure where she was coming from. Her satisfaction at her little show of defiance ebbed drastically once they were in the car, however, and the magnetic pull of his big, powerful body took full sway over her senses.

'You look very beautiful tonight.' His voice was as cool and controlled as always but she caught a husky edge to it that had her glancing into his dark face. His expression was implacable and she could read nothing in it but as he looked back at her, just for a lightning moment, the brilliant intensity of his eyes made her breath catch in her throat.

Why did he want to marry her? she asked herself silently. Was it just because she fitted some preconceived idea he'd had of what his future wife, the mother of his children, had to be like?

She imagined the weight of his powerful body holding her prisoner, his hands and mouth moving over the softness of her feminine curves and felt weak with a strange mixture of excitement and fear and a hundred other emotions that flushed her skin and made her unutterably glad that he couldn't read her mind.

She had never thought, even in her wildest dreams, that she could feel this way about a man she didn't love but then Carlton was no ordinary man. The poor excuse for her annoying weakness was unsatisfactory and she knew it.

'You can return the compliment, you know.' His voice was mocking now, dry and sardonic, and that made it easier for her to respond in like vein.

'You want me to say you're beautiful?' she asked in tones of exaggerated surprise.

'It'd be a start.' He shot her a glance of derisive cynicism. 'Frankly, I'd take anything I could get at the moment.'

'I'm sure your ego is quite big enough as it is,' she said tartly. 'It doesn't need any help from me.'

'Oh, it does, Katie.' There was a rueful note in the deep voice now. 'I hate to disappoint you but I'm only human, you know.'

'You don't seem it half the time.' The moment the words had left her lips she regretted them, thinking that they would spoil the evening before it had started, but surprisingly he didn't fire back with a caustic rejoinder. Instead he pulled the car off the road into a quiet, gated pull-in and cut the engine as he turned to face her.

'Don't I?' His hand tilted her chin as he looked deep into her eyes. 'Then that is my misfortune, perhaps, because I assure you I am very human, Katie. I bleed when I'm cut and I feel pain as keenly as the next man.'

'But you wouldn't let anyone see like the next man might,' she whispered tremblingly as his hand moved to the nape of her neck and stroked the silky skin gently.

'Ah, now there you might be right...' As his mouth moved over hers in a kiss that was all-consuming she felt almost as though she was melting into the hard male body pressed against hers, but within moments she was free as he moved fully into his own seat and the big car growled into life.

'I've booked a table for half-past eight,' he said quietly, his tone so matter-of-fact that she could have kicked him.

He was an impossible man! She studied him from under her eyelashes as the car moved away. Every time she thought she had a glimmer of insight into that hard, intimidatingly male mind he did or said something that completely destroyed the illusion. And it was beginning to hurt.

Her eyes narrowed as her subconscious tried to bring something to the surface even as her mind rejected the shadow of disquiet. She was in a situation that had been forced upon her; she had had no choice, and all she could do was make the best of things. That was all she was trying to do. She nodded mentally. Just get through as best she could.

Their entrance into the nightclub caused a discreet little ripple of commotion that was not lost on Katie and she knew it was all due to the tall, dark man at her side. The manager appeared at their elbow with a beaming smile as a waiter scurried ahead, almost clearing the way to a table for two in a prime position to one side of the small dance-floor.

She saw that a bottle of champagne was already waiting, nestled in an ice bucket; their chairs were pulled aside for them to be seated with an air of deferential humility and she could almost feel several pairs of female eyes boring into her back as she slid gratefully into her seat.

'OK?' His eyes were dark on her flushed face and she nodded quickly before forcing herself to glance around the room with studied nonchalance. What a place! And what an entrance! Was it always like this with him? For the first time the fact that he was something of a celebrity due to his enormous wealth and power fully registered on her senses. As her gaze travelled full circle she saw that the smoky grey eyes were still trained on her face, their dark depths intuitive. 'You'll have to get used to it, Katie,' he warned her quietly.

'Get used to it?' She didn't like it, this ability of his to read her mind, and there was more than a thread of antagonism in her voice. 'I don't know what you mean.'

'I think you do.' He leaned back in his chair slightly, his eyes speculative. 'There is great interest in my wealth, the significance of which is fuelled almost weekly by people like Jennifer writing their rubbish in the tabloids.' The deep voice was bitingly acidic. 'Now, other than become a recluse, the prospect of which does not appeal in the slightest, the only option open to me is to live life exactly the way I want to, ignoring that which can be ignored.'

'And that which can't?' she asked quietly as she looked into the hard, handsome face opposite with a little shiver.

'Is dealt with.' His eyes had a flinty coldness that chilled her blood. 'I don't go looking for trouble, Katie, but I can deal with it when I have to.'

She didn't doubt it. Not for a minute.

'I see.' She kept all shadow of apprehension out of her voice.

'Not yet, perhaps,' he said grimly, 'but you will. As my wife you will come under my protection but unfortunately the tentacles of the media are pernicious. You will learn to say little and be on your guard—'

'Wonderful,' she interrupted wryly. 'It looks like all this is going to be a bundle of laughs. I take it Jennifer is included in this strategy?' she asked carefully.

'Especially Jennifer.' He raised sardonic black eyebrows. 'Your sister is a barracuda on two legs, in case you hadn't noticed. It is fortunate that the two of you have little to do with each other, although having her in the immediate family is a problem I could well do without.'

'Then why—?' She caught herself up abruptly and subsided back in her seat, aware that she had been about to ask the question that had been tormenting her for days but had become more urgent since her conversation with Joseph earlier that day. The knowledge of that other love burnt like fire at the back of her mind.

'You would like me to open the champagne now, Mr Reef?' She could almost have kissed the portly little manager who appeared at their side again, complete with two massive menus, which he handed to them with elaborate ceremony before proceeding to open the champagne and fill their glasses with the sparkling, effervescent wine that tasted quite wonderful.

Once they were alone again Carlton surveyed her thoughtfully over the top of his menu as she took another sip of the delicious drink. 'I seem to have got something right for a change,' he remarked quietly. 'Champagne is obviously your drink.'

'This particular sort is,' she said appreciatively, 'although, to be honest, I didn't think I liked champagne. I've only had it a couple of times at weddings and so on and it didn't taste anything like this.'

'No—' there was a wry amusement in the dark face as his eyes wandered from her pale, creamy skin to the shining silk of her honey-blonde hair '—it probably wouldn't have. That is a very good vintage that you're guzzling so shamelessly. One advantage of the terrible position you find yourself in is that you won't have to drink mediocre champagne, at least.' The grey eyes were mocking. 'What were you going to say before we were interrupted?'

'Say?' She had hoped he'd forgotten but she might have known that that razor-sharp mind never let anything slip, she thought resentfully as hot colour flooded her face. 'I don't remember—'

'We had been discussing Jennifer and then you asked me why…?' She wasn't going to get away with it. She knew it and he knew it.

'It was nothing.' She lowered her eyes to her menu, raising it so that her face was hidden from his gaze as she searched her mind for something to say that wouldn't suggest that she was in any way interested in either his love life or what he thought of her.

'Katie…' The deep voice was insultingly patient. 'In the short time I've known you you have never opened your mouth without *something* emerging,' he said softly. 'Now spit it out.' She saw him wave the waiter away as he approached for their order and knew her last pretext for hesitating was gone.

'I just wondered, in view of your disliking Jennifer and everything…' She found it hard to continue as the dark eyes held hers, and took a deep, hidden breath before speaking the thought that had been stinging unbearably since the mention of his first love's name. 'I just wondered why you wanted to go ahead with the marriage,' she finished in a little rush, lifting the glass of champagne as he leant back in his seat, his face expressionless, and finishing the contents in two gulps.

'I'm not marrying Jennifer.' He looked devastatingly handsome, she thought helplessly, the dark evening suit a perfect foil for his particular brand of harsh maleness, the dangerous attractiveness that was an essential part of him accentuated by the formal clothes.

'But there must have been other women with fewer complications?' she asked hesitantly, her heart thudding as he watched her so carefully. 'I mean—'

'I know what you mean,' he assured her drily, his tone almost bored. 'But I've already told you, a pretty little socialite with nothing in her head but pound signs doesn't fit the bill for what I have in mind.'

'You don't seem to have had any such compunction in the past from what I've heard,' she said tartly as aching hurt and furious anger at her own vulnerability made her voice tight.

'That's enough.' The easy, bored façade was ripped apart in an instant as he leant forward, his voice low and cold but his eyes fiery. 'If you will listen to rumours and gossip, Katie, then don't expect to hear anything good. Of course I have had relationships with women. At my age I think there would be more justification for anxiety on your part if I hadn't, don't you?' he queried softly with cutting mockery.

'However, if only half of what has been printed about me were true I'd have long ago burnt myself out, and I can assure you I haven't.' The glittering eyes held her own wide ones as if in a steel vice. 'As you will discover in due course.'

He settled back in his seat again as an almost visible mask settled back in place, hiding his thoughts and emotions. 'Now, the poor waiter is getting restless. What would you like to eat?'

In spite of the shaky beginning, halfway through the evening Katie was surprised to find that she was beginning to relax. The food was superb, the service faultless and the clientele... She found herself holding her breath as yet another well-known name, the third in as many minutes, strolled into the dimly lit nightclub. 'Isn't that...?'

'Blake Andrews?' Carlton's voice was smiling and as she turned to him she saw that his face was lit with unconcealed amusement at her wide-eyed enthraldom, and the cynical mockery that was usually evident in the dark face for once was totally absent. 'Yes, it is. I'll introduce you later if you like.'

'You know him?' she asked quietly, hearing the breathless note in her voice with a feeling of self-disgust. He must think that she was so naïve, so stupid, but this place, this whole scene, was so overwhelming that she couldn't disguise the effect it was having on her nervous system.

'Not intimately,' he drawled lazily. 'But Blake is the sort of entertainer who is always pleased to meet a fan, especially one who is both young and beautiful.'

Although the teasing was light, playful even, it hit a raw spot and she flushed violently, lowering her eyes immediately to her glass. Why was she forever destined to make a fool of herself in front of this man? she asked herself painfully.

'Katie?' His hand covered hers as he leant forward. 'Look at me.' She raised eyes that were jade-green with chagrin to stare into grey ones that were soft with an emotion she couldn't name. 'Be yourself.' It was an order and spoken with a quiet intensity that made her hold her breath. 'I can't—' He hesitated as though searching for the right words. 'I can't drop the habits of a lifetime in a few

weeks—they're too deep and too strong—but I'm not trying to humiliate you. Do you believe that?'

'Yes.' It was a whisper but he heard the note of bewildered surprise as she voiced what was obviously the truth
and was satisfied, leaning back in his seat again as he surveyed her through narrowed grey eyes.

'There isn't a woman in this place to touch you tonight,'
he said softly. 'I mean that.'

She couldn't respond; it was taking all her control, all
the fortitude she had built up through the long years since
her mother's death to cope with the knowledge that had
suddenly burst into her consciousness as though his words
had been a key that had unlocked a door she had kept
tightly bolted.

She loved him.

As she forced a careful smile to her face and took a small
sip of champagne her mind was screaming the truth at her.
Quite when this physical attraction, the fascination she had
felt since the first moment of seeing him had changed into
something deeper she didn't know, but she had been fighting the knowledge for days, weeks even. How could she
have been such a fool as to let it happen?

'Katie? Are you all right?' he asked quietly.

She stood up quickly as he spoke, keeping the smile in
place even as the muscles in her jaw hurt with the effort.
'Fine, just fine. I'm just popping to the cloakroom for a
moment; I won't be long.' She had left the table even as
she spoke.

He was too knowledgeable, too intuitive for her to remain sitting there. She found the ladies' cloakroom and
collapsed on to one of the velvet-covered seats in front of
an ornate mirror, overwhelmingly thankful that she had the
small room to herself.

The worst thing, the very worst thing in the world had
happened and she was powerless to do anything about it.

She looked deep into the haunted eyes staring back at her from the mirror and shook her head wearily as she let the truth permeate her mind. Most women would have given everything they possessed to be in her place—the fiancée of Carlton Reef. And the fact that she loved him? They would look on that as natural, inevitable even with a man like him who was larger than life in every way.

But he didn't love *her*. The face in the mirror could offer no comfort. He had made that perfectly clear. A deep sexual attraction, a satisfaction in the type of woman she was and her standards and morals maybe, but that wasn't love. She had experienced years and years of trying to win the love of one cold, ruthless, hard man and had never won. And now the process was to begin again but intensified a million times because what she felt for Carlton made any other emotion in the past seem lukewarm by comparison.

What was she going to do? She groaned and leant her head against the cool glass, only to straighten almost immediately as the door opened and two women, elegance personified, glided past her in a cloud of expensive perfume. That was the sort of woman Carlton should have married.

She watched them in the glass as they purred and wriggled, stroking already immaculate hair and glossing beautiful lips like two sleek, expensive cats. They would know how to survive with a man like him but her sense of self-worth, already badly damaged by her father's constant rejection, was too fragile to endure a life of walking on eggshells.

She bit her lip as the women disappeared and she was left alone again. Stop it. She glared into the greeny brown eyes as she spoke the words again out loud. 'Stop it.' She was going to be his wife, bear his children, be at his side both publicly and privately. And he had said, promised, that there would be no other women.

She would make him love her. Somehow, even if it took years, she would reach that cold, cynical heart and make it her own. Time, if nothing else, was on her side.

aloud, disdaining a rose, which fell to the floor in a velvet
panic, scattering in a little heap at her feet.

"Katie?" Her father came carefully down the stairs, his
arms shaky but steady, and she glanced up at him as she
knelt to collect the spilt petals. "I'll come and talk to
you for a while."

CHAPTER SEVEN

THE next three weeks sped by in a whirl of last-minute
arrangements and minor panics. May had been a beautiful
month, full of warm spring sunshine that heralded the approach of a perfect summer, new life bursting out in a
frenzy of curling new leaves, the heady perfume of a thousand spring flowers, and, best of all, the steady, reassuring
improvement in her father's health that meant the world to
Katie. And she was miserable. Desperately, frantically miserable.

She couldn't fault Carlton's handling of their relationship. He was attentive, affectionate to a point, introducing
her to many facets of his life and work in easy stages so
that she absorbed each one without too much effort, but...

Her brow wrinkled as she arranged a bowl of fresh dawn-
pink roses which she had just picked from the garden, their
rich perfume scenting the hall with their promise of summer.

He was remote, in the same way he had been since that
night they had brought her father home. It was as though
he was deliberately keeping her at a distance, controlling
his emotions in a way she found impossible. His lovemaking was still intoxicating—he only had to touch her for her
to melt in a heady, trembling fever that she strove to con-
ceal—but even in that, or perhaps especially in that, he
allowed himself to go so far and no further, his control
absolute.

And tomorrow she would become his wife in the eyes
of God and man. She stifled the flood of panic as her hands

127

shook, dislodging a rose, which fell to the floor, its velvet petals scattering in a little arc at her feet.

'Katie?' Her father came carefully down the stairs, his steps slow but steady, and she glanced up at him as she knelt to gather the petals in her hand. 'Come and talk to me for a while.'

Since his graduation from the study to his bedroom up-stairs, her father seemed to have accepted that he was really going to get well and the realisation had made life easier for the rest of the White household.

'Come on.' David held out his hand as she rose, and led her into the drawing-room, walking through the wide French doors, open to the early June sunshine, and into the garden beyond, drawing her down beside him on the old wooden bench just behind the house. 'Jennifer will be here soon and that will be the end of any peace and quiet,' he remarked with his customary causticity.

'You don't like peace and quiet,' she chided softly as she smiled up into his face. 'Look at you this week, sorting through all your papers, discussing the business with Carlton all the time, and working into the night when you should be in bed.'

'I'm going to let Carlton run it in future, Katie.' She stared at him, too surprised to speak. 'Or, at least, he's putting one of his managers in to do the job. I'll still be around in an advisory capacity but the heat will be taken out of the job.'

'And that's what you want?' she asked quietly, her eyes fixed on his. 'That's what you really want?'

'Katie...' He paused and, to her amazement, reached out and took both of her hands in his, his eyes soft. 'I've been doing a lot of thinking over the last few weeks when I've been laid up in that damn bed and I've made a hell of a mess of the last few years, haven't I, girl?' He shook his head slowly. 'A hell of a mess.'

'No, I—'

'Don't deny it, lass. Carlton and I have done some honest talking which I didn't thank him for at the time, but I've faced some personal demons that have been on my back for years. I've only loved two people in my life, Katie— your mother was one of them and you are the other.' His eyes were intense on her face.

She had wanted to hear it, needed to hear it for years, but now the reality left her stunned and speechless, her heart thudding painfully as she stared back at him, her eyes enormous.

'I ought to love Jennifer, I know—she's my own flesh and blood—but I don't.' He shook his head. 'No, I don't.'

'Dad—'

'When your mother died I felt my world had ended. Can you understand that?' He gazed at her and the pain in the pale blue eyes mirrored what her own had been at that time. 'The only way I could cope with it and go on was to shut it away, ignore it,' he continued quietly. 'But you were there, Katie, the very image of your mother in your ways and emotions, a kindred spirit, a constant reminder of all I'd lost, and so I shut you out too. Not consciously—I didn't realise I was doing it—but I did it nevertheless. Can you forgive an old fool, lass?' He shook his head slowly. 'Because I can't forgive myself,' he finished with a break in his voice.

'Oh, Dad…' She turned into his arms and he hugged her close, the tears that were streaming down his face wetting her hair as she lay against his chest, her heart full and her eyes moist.

'I want to see my grandchildren, Katie, for your mother as well as myself. I want to make up to you for all the years I've wasted.'

'Dad…' She drew herself back slightly and looked into

his face, her own wet with her tears. 'There's nothing to make up for. I love you—I've always loved you.'

'Coals of fire.' He drew her to him again and sighed deeply, his voice husky. 'I'm a hard man, lass. Your mother knew that when she married me but she still went through with it, bless her. Because she loved me as I loved her. Katie—' he moved to look into her upturned face '—do you love Carlton? Really love him?'

'Yes.' In this, at least, she could be honest even if the reason for their marriage had to remain forever hidden. She took a deep breath and smiled through her tears. 'I do love him.'

'That's all I wanted to know.' He settled her against him, the June sunshine warm on their faces. 'I know he loves you—what man wouldn't?—but it's important for a woman to feel absolutely sure, with everything that the physical side of a marriage entails. You know what I mean?' he added uncomfortably.

'Yes, Dad.' Her face hidden from his gaze, she smiled at the touch of fatherly advice, but in the next instant the smile disappeared as Jennifer's voice sounded from within the house, high and authoritative and strident.

'Here we go.' He straightened, moving her gently to one side, but it didn't hurt at all. She knew how he felt now. That was all that mattered. She didn't need effusive shows of affection.

'I know he loves you—what man wouldn't?' The irony of his words stayed with her all that morning and into the afternoon, when, her father having retired for his afternoon nap, Jennifer dragged her into her bedroom so that she could watch her try on her bridesmaid's dress again.

'Do you think the colour is really me?'

As her sister turned and pirouetted in front of the mirror, the deep wine-red of the dress swirling round her feet in a cloud of silk, Katie stifled an irritated sigh. Jennifer hadn't once asked about her father's health, the state of their finances, even any details about the wedding except those directly concerning her.

'It's the dress you chose,' she said patiently. 'We went through the whole shop if you remember.'

'And what a shop...' Jennifer gave one more twirl and then reluctantly took the beautiful dress off and replaced it on its hanger. 'I've got to hand it to you, Katie, you've got your head screwed on all right. I used to wonder—but to make a catch like Carlton Reef must have taken some planning.'

'Planning?' Katie stared at her sister with distaste. 'I didn't plan anything.'

'Oh, come on.' Jennifer laughed unpleasantly. 'He's had more women than I've had hot dinners and his mistress is really something, as you probably know. You can't tell me that this all happened by accident. You'll have to give me some advice on—'

'What do you mean, "mistress"?' Katie asked through suddenly numb lips, her blood freezing in her veins.

'Whoops!' Jennifer's slanted eyes narrowed still more as she placed her hand over her mouth in affected horror. 'You mean to say you didn't know? I'd have thought that he'd at least have told you...'

'Told me what?' She wanted to walk out of the room, pretend she was unaffected by the malicious envy that was suddenly so apparent in Jennifer's almond-shaped eyes, but she was held rooted to the floor by some power stronger than herself. 'I don't believe there's anything to tell,' she said flatly, her stomach churning.

'About his mistress or all the other women?' Jennifer asked with catty innocence. 'Well, I can assure you it's all true. One advantage of my job is that I get to know all the inside titbits...

'Carlton has been keeping a woman in a flat in Mayfair

for several years now although it's all supposed to be hush-hush. They're never seen out in public together but then she probably serves a more useful purpose inside, if you know what I mean,' she said with crude spitefulness. 'And he's still had other women on the side; the man must have a voracious appetite.' The pale blue eyes narrowed further. 'But then you'd know all about that—or would you, my sweet, virginal little sister?'

Katie ignored the obvious question as she turned away, her legs trembling and the blood pounding so violently in her ears that she felt dizzy. 'It's not true,' she whispered. 'I don't believe it. You're just jealous.'

'Too true, sweetie; I've never tried to hide it. I—' As Katie turned back to face her something in her eyes caught Jennifer's words in her throat and for a moment she looked acutely uncomfortable.

'Oh, don't take it like that, Katie. What did you expect anyway? He's hardly a shy little flower, is he? Look, perhaps I've got it wrong,' she added urgently as Katie sank down on the bed, her legs finally giving way. 'Perhaps this woman is—is—' She ran out of words. 'A friend,' she finished, with a wry, embarrassed little laugh. 'Anyway, he's marrying you. That's more than enough, isn't it? All the women I know are pea-green—'

'What's her name?' Katie asked flatly. 'This woman, what's her name?'

'I don't know.'

'You know.' Katie looked hard into the beautiful face in front of her. 'You're a good reporter, Jennifer—you find out all the sordid details before you let rip,' she accused bitterly.

Jennifer tossed her head, the tone of Katie's voice erasing all guilt from her face. 'A Mrs Staples. Penny Staples. She used to be a model before Carlton took up with her but then she dropped out of sight. Perhaps he didn't want her working or seeing other men; I don't know. She's the original recluse now, anyway, but Carlton pays the rent each year; that much I do know for sure. And I thought it was my duty to make sure you knew,' she added tartly. 'We are sisters after all.'

'Yes, we are sisters,' Katie agreed dully as she rose slowly and left the room, her heart thudding so hard that it was a physical pain. Penny. *Penny*. It was too much of a coincidence for it not to be the same Penny whom Joseph had told her about. So he had loved her all these years, biding his time until he could persuade her to belong to him again. But why hadn't he married her?

The thudding had transferred itself to her head now and she felt nauseous as she collapsed on to her own bed after locking the door. Perhaps she was already married; perhaps the 'Mrs' was real? Or maybe...

She sat up, the room spinning, as another thought occurred to her. Perhaps he had some hold on her too? Something that had forced her to leave the catwalk and all the glamour and allow herself to be incarcerated in what virtually amounted to a prison, just waiting for the moments when he could spare her some time and ease her solitude. Was it some form of weird punishment? A form of retribution for a love he couldn't let go?

And Maisie? The pain in her heart was so fierce that it was catching her breath. How did she fit into the scheme of things? Her knowing about his mistress suddenly made the close relationship Carlton had with the beautiful brunette even more suspect. She felt that there was something between them, some secret; she had felt it all along but had tried to put it out of her mind. Perhaps she was his mistress too? A hundred little incidents she had noticed but dismissed returned to her mind with renewed vigour. He was so different with Maisie in a way she couldn't quite pinpoint.

When the tears came in a burning, blinding flood they didn't help. Even after she had cried herself dry the ache in her heart was savage. She lay on her bed, careless of all the hundred and one things she still had left to do, and watched the afternoon sky with blind eyes until the bedside clock told her it was five o'clock. He would be home now and she had to go and see him, confront him with the truth and tear away all the lies and meaningless promises he had made. 'Absolute fidelity'. She clenched her teeth and forced back the sudden rush of tears before washing her face and fixing her hair into a knot high on top of her head. When she faced him she wanted to be cool and controlled—an ice woman to match the ice man.

Jennifer was waiting in the hall when she ventured downstairs. From the pile of magazines by her side it looked as though she had been there all afternoon. 'I told Mrs Jenkins you had a headache and wanted to sleep,' she whispered nervously as Katie reached her side and picked up her car keys. 'And where on earth do you think you're going now?'

'Where do you think?' Katie asked dully.

'I wouldn't—'

'I'm not interested in what you would or wouldn't do.' Jennifer was still standing in the hall open-mouthed as she left the house. She had never spoken to her in such a cold tone before. Perhaps she should have done so a long time ago.

Carlton was in his study when Maisie led her through and as he looked up from his desk, his face breaking into one of his rare smiles when he saw her framed in the doorway, she knew a rage so strong that she had to restrain herself from leaping at his face like a wild animal. How dared he smile at her like that when all the time—?

'Katie?' His smile faded at the look on her face and as

Maisie shut the door, leaving them alone, he rose swiftly from the desk. 'What's wrong? Is it David?'

'My father is fine.' Something in her voice brought him to a halt just in front of her, the arms that had reached out dropping back by his sides as he looked down at her. 'Who is Penny Staples?' she asked with icy control, and as she saw the blow register in his eyes she knew that Jennifer hadn't been lying, and the last tiny scrap of hope died.

'I don't know what you've heard, Katie, but I can explain.' He motioned her to the seat facing his desk but she remained standing, her eyes set tightly on his face. 'Penny is an old friend—'

'The old friend you were going to marry once?' she asked acidly, willing the anger to hold the trembling that was threatening to take over and render her useless. '*That* old friend?'

'Someone has been very busy.' The surge of angry red colour that fired his high cheekbones didn't intimidate her at all—she was way, way past that. 'Dare I make a guess that Jennifer is home?' he asked coldly. 'The fount of all knowledge?'

'Do you keep an old friend in a flat in Mayfair?' she spat at him as she felt her control slipping and the urge to scream and tear at him with her hands grow. 'And I want the truth, Carlton,' she warned bitterly.

'Sit down, Katie.' As she still stood swaying in the middle of the room he reached out and forced her into the seat, only to have her spring up and away from him as his hands left her shoulders.

'Don't you touch me.' So great was her rage that she hit her hip on the corner of his desk and didn't feel a thing. 'I want to know about your mistress, Carlton—this old, old friend.'

'She is not my mistress.' The words were punched out into the room as he watched her through narrowed eyes. 'I can explain it all if you'll just sit in the damn chair and listen to me. Penny and I were close once but that was a long time ago—'

'And she left you for someone else.' Katie stared at him, seeing all her tentative hopes for the future crashing down about her ears. 'I know that. All I want to know now is if you pay the rent for her flat in Mayfair.'

'Yes.' His eyes never left her face as he spoke. 'I pay the rent. I was going to explain it all when we had some time alone together in Spain after the wedding, when I could make you understand.'

'I'll never understand.' She drew herself up as her heart slowly broke, and faced him with an icy composure that was the result of shock and pain. 'I hate you, Carlton Reef. I thought that at least you would keep your word in this monstrous farce of a relationship but I might have known you would run true to type. You disgust me; everything about you disgusts me.' She was lashing out through her own bitter hurt and humiliation, trying to scourge the love from her heart with cruel words and an icy front, but inside she was screaming, dying.

'I know that.' As his control broke he leapt at her so savagely that her head jerked back on her shoulders when he caught her arms in his hands, shaking her like a dog with a bone. 'Don't you think I don't know that?' he snarled rawly, his eyes glittering with an unholy fire and his face black with rage. 'I've felt the way you tense every time I so much as lay a finger on you, seen the reproach and wariness in those damn great eyes every time you look at me. I *know* how you feel, Katie.

'You were just waiting for something like this, weren't you—some excuse to get out of the commitment you made of your own free will?' He shook her again, his eyes lethal. 'You wouldn't unbend an inch, damn you. I've been turning inside out trying to keep to the softly-softly approach, to show you I'm not quite the animal you seem to imagine. I thought you'd begin to understand, that I could show you—' He made an exclamation of disgust as he threw her to one side.

'I've been trying not to come on too heavy, to frighten you, and where has it got me?' He swore, softly and succinctly, as his eyes washed over her white face.

'This is not my fault—'

He cut short her protestation with a bark of a laugh that grated harshly. 'I didn't say it was.'

Before she knew what he was going to do he had closed the gap between them, gripping her wrists as he hauled her against the hard wall of his body with ruthless ease. 'And you know the thing that really has been driving your ice-cool brain crazy, the thing you couldn't forgive me for?' he asked thickly as he looked down into her trapped eyes. 'You want me. Physically you want me as much as I want you. You might not like to hear that, my cold, suspicious little fiancée, but we both know I could have had you at any time over the last few weeks and you would have been there all the way.'

'No—' As he took her mouth in a fierce, contemptuous kiss that forced her head back she was conscious of one piercing moment of thankfulness that he hadn't guessed the truth—that she loved him—and then all her energy went into fighting him. The cold control of the previous weeks had melted like ice before fire and the raw, primitive desire that had him in its grip made him blind and deaf to everything but his own need as he sated his passion on her twisting form.

She was moulded into his body, the evidence of his desire hard and fierce against her softness, and although she fought him with all her strength he hardly seemed to notice. And then, through the anger and shock and self-contempt, she felt herself respond to his need as it fired her own passion.

She hated herself even as she trembled against him, all resistance gone; she hated herself for her incurable weakness where he was concerned, but she just couldn't help it. She loved him. It had no rhyme or reason, and he would never understand that it was more than mere physical lust, but she could no more resist him than fly.

As he felt her submission the tempo of his assault changed, his mouth immediately persuasive and sensual as he kissed her throat and ears, his hands removing her light blouse with experienced ease before she even realised what he was doing, and cupping her full breasts in their brief lacy covering, his thumbs running over their swollen peaks. She gasped, her body alive with sensation after sensation as he continued to kiss and caress her, making her tremble with hungry expectancy.

She wanted him—she needed him… Through the maelstrom of tormenting desire that thought was uppermost. But like this? After what she had just discovered? Where was her pride? Her self-respect? But even as the warning formed it was gone in a turmoil of touch and taste, his devastating experience and knowledge in the sensual arts combining with her love to render her helpless and quivering in his arms.

'Now do you doubt it?' Suddenly, shockingly, the warmth of his body had left hers and she almost whimpered with the betrayal. He held her at arm's length, desire turning his eyes into glittering black onyx, his face hard and set. 'I won't take you until we are legally married—that's one thing at least you won't be able to accuse me of—but tomorrow you *will* become mine, Katie. Do you understand that?'

She was unable to speak, staring at him with great bruised eyes as he bent and retrieved her blouse from the floor. 'Put it on.' She struggled into the cotton material hastily, her cheeks burning, but when it came to fastening the small pearl buttons her fingers wouldn't obey. He watched her fumble for a few moments and then brushed her hands aside, doing up the tiny buttons with perfectly steady hands, his face expressionless.

'I hate you.' And for an infinitesimal moment she did. How could he stand there, with that iron control firmly in place once more, and act almost as though this was all her fault? It just wasn't fair. None of this was fair. He had things all his own way, far more than he realised.

The sting of tears at the back of her eyes brought her head up sharply and straightened her trembling mouth. Oh, no, she would have none of that. No tears in front of him.

'I think we can take that as read,' he said grimly. 'But you are going to sit and listen to me, Katie, whether you like it or not.' He indicated the chair with an abrupt nod of his head. '*Now*. You are making an appearance at that church tomorrow come hell or high water and I'm not giving you an excuse to change your mind because nothing has altered—nothing at all.'

She sat. There was nothing else she could do and, besides, she had the awful suspicion that if she didn't she would collapse at his feet as the trembling that was situated at the very core of her body threatened to take over.

'As your evil-minded sister informed you, I do pay the rent on an apartment which Penny Staples occupies,' he continued coldly as he walked round the desk and sat down facing her in the massive leather chair he had been occupying before she had interrupted him. 'But she is not my mistress.'

As she twisted restlessly in her chair, half rising, he motioned her back with a sharp wave of his hand, his voice a bark. 'Sit, damn you! You've made one hell of an accusation tonight and you will listen to me even if I have to tie you in that chair. Now…'

He took a deep, shuddering breath and she realised, for the first time, that he wasn't quite as in control as he would have liked her to believe. It helped—not a lot—but it gave her the courage to sit still and watch his face silently as he talked.

'As I said, I intended to tell you about Penny on our honeymoon when I'd made you understand how I—' He stopped abruptly and shook his head, rising from his seat to stand with his back towards her as he looked out of the window into the mellow evening sunshine.

'I knew Penny from my university days,' he continued flatly, 'and, as your informant's already told you, we'd planned to get married one day. Then the accident changed everything. Suddenly I had the responsibility of my father's businesses and all that that entailed, plus a badly hurt younger brother who needed all my spare time and attention. Penny didn't like it.'

He paused for a moment and she saw the broad back stiffen. 'The final break came when I went round to her flat one night thinking to surprise her and found her in bed with a friend of mine. It was a surprise all right,' he added grimly. 'I called her all the names under the sun and left and that was that. But I felt bitter, very bitter, for a long, long time.

'Joe stabilised. I found I had a flair for business and everything I touched turned to gold, and I made sure my private life was run exactly the way I wanted it. On my terms. No commitment, no promises; I took what I wanted when I wanted it and if they didn't like it they could always walk. Not very pretty but that's how it was.'

'And Penny?' she asked stiffly, the pain that had flooded her heart at the thought of those other women keeping her back straight.

'She'd become a model—a successful one,' he said slowly. 'A different guy for each new outfit—that sort of lifestyle. I'd seen her around at a distance but then one night about five years after the split, she came across to my table in a crowded nightclub and we talked about old times. She laid it on the line; she wanted me back.'

He paused. 'But there was nothing there—nothing. It had taken me all that time to realise the girl I thought I'd loved was a figment of my imagination, an illusion. It scared me to death. How could I have been so mistaken? I'd have *married* the girl, for crying out loud. So I became even more determined that any relationship I had would be on my terms, that this so-called love was merely a short-lived feeling in one's imagination that died as quickly as it was given life.'

'But the apartment?' she asked bewilderedly. 'If you don't love her...'

'I haven't slept with Penny Staples since I was twenty-three years old,' he said coolly as he looked straight into her eyes, a shaft of sunlight from the window behind him turning his hair fiery black. 'But five years ago I got a call from a London hospital to say they'd got a patient who had tried to commit suicide, had no next of kin and had given my name as the only contact. It was Penny. I went to see her and she was in a mess.'

He shook his head slowly. 'She had skin cancer, badly; she'd left it far too late to do anything about it because she was scared an operation might ruin her looks for the mod-elling circuit. What would have been a small scar on her jaw ended up as a major operation to remove half her face.'

'Carlton...' As her face whitened he nodded slowly.

'I know. She had no friends, no money; her looks were gone and she wanted to die. But I wouldn't let her. Rightly or wrongly I wouldn't let her. The plastic surgeons did what they could but the results weren't good. But one thing came out of all the months of hospitalisation—she found she could paint. Water-colours. They're damn good too.

'So I provided the apartment when she was well enough to leave and she supports herself in everything else with her painting. She has a few close friends now among the artist community and is content in her own way, although she never leaves the apartment. Her life is her painting, her friends and her two cats.'

'Do you visit her?' she asked painfully, her head whirling. Whatever she had thought, it wasn't this. 'To see how she is, I mean.'

'Occasionally.' He gestured abruptly with his hand. 'She asked for my help knowing I didn't love her and that she didn't love me. It was an appeal from the past, in memory of two young kids who had fun for a time before it all went sour. And it was in that vein that I responded.

'There is nothing there beyond a strange feeling of duty, not even friendship, but I couldn't have turned my back on her when she had nothing and no one. And the financial side is a drop in the ocean to me but means security and stability to her. I'd have done the same for anyone in that position.'

'I see.' She rubbed a shaking hand across her eyes before rising to face him. 'I'm sorry, Carlton; I made a terrible mistake. But I didn't know.'

'No one does.' He shrugged slowly. 'Penny didn't want anyone to know about her face and what had happened. The world is cruel but the modelling world even more so and the media would have had a field day for a time until some other poor so-and-so took their attention.

'She just disappeared from sight, changed her name to Staples, added the ''Mrs'' and cauterised the wound of her old life. Her artist friends have no idea who she was previously but they're a good bunch—they don't care. How did Jennifer find out about it?' he asked abruptly. 'I presume it was Jennifer?'

'Yes.' She stared at him miserably, loving him more than she would have thought possible and terrified that he might read it in her face. 'I don't know how she found out but she is jealous about—about us,' she finished painfully. 'I suppose, knowing Jennifer, she dug and dug away until she got something; she has contacts you wouldn't dream of.'

'Oh, yes, I would,' he said grimly.

'And since Penny you've never fallen in love again?' She had to ask now, while he was actually talking to her. She had been wrong about Penny, criminally wrong, but there was still Maisie and, by his own admission, several other liaisons through the years. She had to know it all, face the worst now.

'I—' He had been facing her, his face taut and strained, but as she asked the question something flickered in the smoky depths of his eyes for an instant and he hesitated before turning to look out of the window again. 'Why do you ask?'

'Because—' Because I love you, I can't live without you, I'm going to marry you tomorrow knowing you don't love me, but you've reduced me to this creature who will take anything she can get, she thought wildly. 'Because it's only fair that I know,' she continued bleakly. 'You know everything about me—not that there was anything much to know,' she added bitterly.

'Yes, I see.' She saw him straighten, as though he had taken a deep breath, before he faced her again. 'Do you want me to be honest?' he asked with a grim seriousness that stopped her heart.

'Of course I do.' She stared at him, sheer will-power keeping her face cool and still and her eyes veiled.

'Are you sure?' he asked heavily. 'You might not like what you hear.'

'I want to know.' Her heart was thudding so hard that she was sure he must be able to hear it.

'Then the answer has to be yes,' he said tiredly. 'Yes, I have. I think you've known for some time deep down inside, haven't you?'

'Oh.' If the world had stopped spinning at that moment she wouldn't have cared. It was Maisie; it had to be. All the hundred and one little incidents from the past, the tender gestures, the gentleness, the innate kindness. It had to be the beautiful, shy brunette.

But why couldn't he marry her? What was stopping him from taking her as his wife? Didn't she return his love? Perhaps they hadn't been lovers. Perhaps Maisie had held him at a distance, unable to love him in return except as a friend. Or was there an obstacle she knew nothing about?

'And now you've had it confirmed.' He stared at her across the room, his eyes holding hers as her face registered her awareness. 'And it hasn't helped, as I knew it wouldn't. You're more shocked, more panicky——'

'I have to go.' She spoke through numb lips as she backed from him, the look on his face piercing her heart like a sword. She didn't want to hear more—hear the details about another woman who had captured his cold heart for her own. She wouldn't be able to bear it. What good would it do anyway?

She knew now that she would marry him tomorrow whether or not he gave help to her father. She would marry him because she loved him, because a life without him in it would be pointless and empty and cold, even as a life as his wife would be an unending torment of pain and grief. But it would be better than knowing he was alive somewhere, walking and talking on this planet without her.

'Katie——' As he took a step towards her she found her hand on the doorknob and wrenched open the door savagely.

'No, don't come near me.' She couldn't bear to hear more. 'I'll be there tomorrow—you have my word—but I need to go home now.' And as she slammed the door behind her, a sob catching in her throat, it was as though she was slamming a door on all her hopes and dreams.

CHAPTER EIGHT

SHE was a beautiful bride—everyone said so—but as Katie drifted through the day on Carlton's arm—the ceremony, the reception—it was as though it were all a dream, indistinct and unreal. She knew her father was worried about her but she couldn't seem to find the words through the fog in her mind to reassure him, although she caught him looking at her time and time again, his pale blue eyes narrowed with concern.

There was dancing after the meal at the lavish hotel that Carlton had booked for the reception and as he raised her to her feet, the guests clapping as they took the floor, she felt her footsteps falter, and in the same instant his hand came firmly round her waist. 'Don't faint on me, little wife.' His eyes were glittering with some dark emotion as he looked into the speckled light of hers. 'See it through to the bitter end.'

Her eyes were wide and dazed as they looked into his, her skin a pale, translucent cream that complemented the ivory silk dress with its mass of tiny seed-pearls and old lace, the skirt wide and hooped and the bodice fitting like a glove. 'I'm not going to faint,' she said quietly, the tiara of tiny pink rosebuds in her hair reflecting the colour of her pale lips. 'I told you once before, I've never fainted in my life.'

'And I called you formidable.' He looked down at her as they began to dance, the full skirt of her dress preventing close contact. 'I had no idea then just how formidable.'

'Formidable?' She stared up at him in bewilderment. He

146

thought this mass of bruised emotion and trembling flesh that he held in his arms 'formidable'?

'You don't think so?' he asked softly as her face mirrored her thoughts. 'Innocence is a terrible weapon, my love; don't ever doubt it.'

'My love'? It was the first time he had used such an endearment and it cut like a knife. She would have given the rest of her life for one hour in his arms with him meaning those two words, she thought painfully.

The revelations of the day before had meant a sleepless night and an aching heart, and as she had sat and watched the night sky change from dark velvet blue to a dawn streaked with pink and orange she wept until there had been no more tears left. The magnificent wedding-dress on its hanger on her wardrobe door had seemed like a mockery then, the fine veil with its intricate lace and pearls an abomination, but she was married now.

She glanced up at him as the music came to an end and their solitary dance finished with the assembled throng clapping and cheering as they began to take to the floor. 'For better for worse, for richer for poorer, in sickness and in health'—

'You are breathtaking.' His eyes were waiting for her glance. 'Ethereal, exquisite, so delicately beautiful I'm afraid you might break.'

'Don't.' It was too much after the day before, spoken as it was in a deep, husky voice that sent shivers down to her toes and made her weak.

'I'm sorry.' His expression instantly hardened into granite, the familiar mask hiding his emotions as he looked away from her and round the crowded dance-floor. 'I didn't realise my mere words would be so distasteful.'

'They aren't.' She didn't know what to say, how to handle this powerful, hard man who could turn from ice to fire and then back again all in the same breath and leave her trembling in confusion. 'It's just that…'

'Just that?' he asked softly, his eyes veiled as he looked down into her troubled face. 'Just that you're frightened, nervous, wondering how you're going to face the night ahead and all the other nights?'

'I didn't say that.'

'Don't be frightened, my formidable little wife. Physically, at least, we will be compatible,' he said thickly. 'I will make you want me as you've never dreamed it possible to want a man, in spite of how you feel about me in the cold light of day. You will tremble in my arms, plead, moan for that which only I can give. I promise you that.'

'Carlton…' She was trembling already, the dark, fiery side of him that she had only glimpsed now and again raw and naked in front of her eyes as his gaze roamed over her face and body with a hunger that was voracious and quite at odds with the very English, formal tailed suit.

'I've wanted you from the moment I saw you,' he whispered softly as the other dancers swirled and moved around them. 'From the second I saw your photograph on David's desk.'

'My photo?' She tried to pull away a little but he was holding her too tightly, his hand like a band of steel on her waist and his body rigid as he crushed her closer against him, careless now of the beautiful dress.

'You were sitting with Jennifer in some park or other and while she laughed into the camera, her face tilted for the best pose, you gazed into the lens like a little lost dove, your eyes wide and beckoning and your hair loose about your shoulders like raw silk. As it will be tonight.' His gaze moved to the tiny curls and waves on top of her head which had taken the hairdresser over an hour to accomplish.

How could he love one woman and want another the way he wanted her? she asked herself bitterly. Were all men like this? Able to detach their bodies so completely from their emotions? Her eyes chilled with resentment and humiliation and she turned her head away, her body stiff and unyielding and her face cold with hidden pain.

'Stop frowning.' The expression on his face as she raised her eyes to his again made her catch her breath. There was hunger there, rage, a strange kind of bitterness and, she would almost have thought, pain. 'This is your wedding-day; you are the radiant bride. At least try to act the part for a few hours, if only for David's benefit.' He gestured with the merest inclination of his head towards her father, sitting at the top table in the distance, and she saw that although he was talking to Joseph his eyes returned every few seconds to her face and his lined face was worried.

From that point she threw herself into the allotted part with all her might, circulating on Carlton's arm and chatting happily with all their guests, her lips smiling, her eyes bright and her nerves stretched to breaking-point. Just before they left the party later that evening she found herself in a quiet corner with David, her facial muscles aching with the effort it had taken to keep the smile in place all day.

'Is everything all right, lass?' He took one of her hands in his as he looked into her face. 'You seem a sight too het up to me.'

'It's my wedding-day, Dad.' She forced a light laugh from somewhere. 'Surely a girl has a right to be excited on her wedding-day?'

'And that's all it is?' he asked quietly. 'There's nothing wrong?'

'Nothing.' If he said much more with that loving look on his face she would burst into tears, she thought frantically, and then all this would be for nothing. He mustn't find out the truth or the price she had paid to give him peace of mind.

'Have you ever seen such a beautiful bride?' Carlton's

deep voice over her shoulder made her sag with relief as her father's eyes moved from her face and up to his.

'Never.' The two men smiled at each other before Carlton's hand under her elbow raised her gently to her feet.

'Time to say our goodbyes, darling,' he said smoothly.

The last twenty minutes seemed the worst but at last it was over and she went upstairs with Jennifer, who was going to help her change in the room that Carlton had reserved, before they left the hotel, where the festivities were going to continue into the early hours.

'You looked lovely today, Katie.' As Jennifer unhooked the tiny buttons at the back of the dress and helped her step out of it, her voice was full of reluctant admiration. 'Things went OK last night, then?' she asked with heavy casualness.

'Yes.' As the flurry of silk and lace was laid on the sofa at her side Katie reached for the simple cream linen dress and jacket she had chosen to wear and slipped into the dress quickly. 'Help me take the flowers out of my hair, would you? This tiara is fixed with a thousand pins; it kept slipping out of my hair without them.'

'You don't want to talk about it?' Jennifer asked quietly.

'No.' Katie turned and looked her sister straight in the eye. 'Not now, not ever. It's OK and I want to leave it at that.'

'Fine, fine.' Jennifer's hands deftly removed the tiara without disturbing the upswept curls. 'I'm sure you know what you're doing,' she said tartly, with a faint trace of spitefulness.

As she left the lift in the reception area a few minutes later, Jennifer just behind her, and caught sight of Carlton, big and dark as he towered over all the other men present, Katie thought that she had never in her life been less sure of what she was doing than right now. She loved him. She ached with love for him and as she walked to his side and he smiled down at her, devastatingly attractive in his dark morning suit, she felt a sudden fierce determination to make things work whatever the cost, to turn this fiasco around and make him if not happy, then at least content.

That spirit of sacrificial nobility lasted exactly five minutes until Carlton shook hands with Joseph, who had been his best man, and then turned to take Maisie in his arms, kissing her gently before whispering something quietly in her ear that made the lovely brunette flush and drop her eyes shyly.

And then they were being showered with confetti as they ran for the car, parked outside the huge glass doors of Reception, and the last goodbyes were said, her bouquet of fresh pink rosebuds and white freesias thrown over her shoulder into the waiting crowd, and the big car with Carlton's chauffeur at the wheel glided away as she waved frantically to her father, the tears that had been threatening to fall all day spilling over at the sight of him standing slightly to one side of the rest of the throng, hand raised in farewell, his eyes suspiciously bright.

'Here.' A large white handkerchief was thrust under her nose as Carlton pulled her into his side with his other arm. 'Just shut your eyes and relax for a while. It's a little way to the hotel where we're spending the night, but I thought it would be better to get right away somewhere where the practical jokers couldn't find us.'

'Yes.' What had he said to Maisie in those last few seconds? she asked herself bitterly as she wiped her eyes, trying not to smudge the delicate eye make-up that the beautician had been so painstaking over earlier in the day. *What had he said?*

It was a full twenty minutes later that the Mercedes glided into the small courtyard in front of a rambling country-style hotel with leaded windows and old, mellow stone.

The smell of wood-smoke was heavy in the dusk-laden air as Carlton helped her from the car.

'What a lovely place.' She forced herself to speak normally, conscious of the chauffeur extracting their cases from the back of the car, and Carlton nodded slowly. They hadn't spoken a word to each other on the drive from the reception, but he had seemed content to sit quietly with his arm around her and her body leaning against his as she had shut her eyes and let her thoughts torment her.

'I thought you'd like it. I've arranged a taxi to pick us up tomorrow morning and take us to the airport. Now...' He turned to the chauffeur and smiled. 'Not a word as to where you brought us, Bob. Joe still has enough of the boy about him to try some damn silly trick.'

'Mum's the word, sir.' The young man grinned at them both conspiratorially. 'I'll let 'em cut my tongue out first.'

'A somewhat extreme expedient but I appreciate the thought,' Carlton responded drily as the three of them walked up the steps and into the small foyer where he was greeted with the normal rapturous welcome that Katie was beginning to expect.

'Would you like dinner served in our room or in the restaurant?' he asked her quietly as Bob and the porter walked to the lift with their cases.

'The restaurant,' Katie said quickly—too quickly. The thought of being alone with him was doing strange things to her insides and the prospect of delaying it a little longer was welcome. She caught the narrowed glance he shot at her but he said nothing, indicating the lift, where Bob and the porter were waiting with the doors open, with a wave of his hand.

'But I thought... I mean—weren't we going to have dinner?' she stammered nervously. 'You said—'

'I thought you would like to freshen up a little before we come down,' Carlton said smoothly as he took her arm and began to lead her towards the waiting lift, but not before she had seen the flash of anger in the smoky grey eyes. The lift travelled upwards silently and once on their floor, which was thickly carpeted and discreetly elegant, the porter led the way to the first door and opened it before handing the key to Carlton and allowing them to walk through.

'Oh, it's beautiful…' They had entered a suite of rooms luxuriously furnished in cream and gold, the air redolent with the perfume from several bowls of fresh flowers, and the full-length windows in the small sitting-room open to the gentle evening breeze that drifted in from the gardens below. Aware that he had thought carefully about their first night together and had tried to please her, she turned impulsively to him as the chauffeur and porter left the room. 'Thank you; it's lovely here,' she said shyly as he looked down at her with unfathomable eyes.

She had expected him to kiss her as soon as they were alone but he merely smiled carefully before walking through to the small bedroom and indicating her overnight case on the huge double bed. 'Would you like me to wait downstairs while you freshen up?' he asked quietly, his back towards her and his voice strangely thick.

'No, no, it's all right,' she said hastily. 'I'll just fix my hair and then we can go down. I won't be a minute.' Nerves made her all fingers and thumbs but just as she finished combing out her hair from the intricate style that the hairdresser had laboured over that morning, and which had been making her head ache for the last few hours, a light touch on her shoulder made her nearly jump out of her skin.

'Dammit, Katie!' Carlton had jumped too at her reaction and now she saw, in the reflection in the dressing-table mirror, that his face was dark with rage. 'What the hell do you think I'm going to do to you? Leap on you at the first opportunity and rip off all your clothes? Credit me with a little finesse at least.'

'I'm sorry.' She rose and turned from the stool where she had been sitting as she spoke, her cheeks pink. 'I'm just tired, I think; it's been a hectic day. I didn't mean...' Her voice dwindled away as she strove to bite back the hot tears at the back of her eyes.

This was awful; everything was awful. Why couldn't he love her? Thousands and millions of really plain women were loved. Was she so unlovable? Couldn't he see the real person under the skin he seemed to desire so much? Why did there have to be a Maisie?

'Don't cry. I can just about stand this if you don't cry,' he said thickly as he reached out and pulled her roughly into his arms, holding her against his chest for a long moment before pushing her away and placing a small box in her hand. 'I just wanted to give you this.' His face seemed to hold a wealth of pain. 'A wedding-gift.'

'But you've paid out so much for me already,' she murmured, meaning nothing beyond that she was grateful for all he'd done for her father, but even as she lifted the lid to the box her eyes still held his and she saw that he had misconstrued her words.

'You're never going to let me forget it, are you?' he ground out savagely through clenched teeth. 'Even though you know how I feel there's going to be no lowering of the drawbridge, dammit.'

How he felt? How did what he felt alter anything? she thought dazedly before she glanced down at the exquisite dark gold locket that the box held, a work of art in intricate, fine, worked gold and delicate engraving that was truly magnificent. 'It was my grandmother's,' Carlton said quietly, his voice smooth and controlled again. 'Open it.'

She flicked the tiny little catch and then froze, staring down at the tiny pictures either side of the hinge. Her mother's face smiled back at her, the minute photograph beautifully sharp and clear, and on the other side her father had his customary scowl which appeared whenever he looked into a camera. She continued staring down at her mother's face, at the photograph she had never seen before and hadn't known existed, as burning tears began to flood down her cheeks and shake her body.

'Katie, Katie, Katie… Don't. Don't feel so intensely; don't hurt so much…' And then she was in his arms again but this time she raised her head to his, searching for his lips, his gesture concerning her mother's picture cutting through all the hurt and pain he had inflicted, was still inflicting, and would continue to inflict. 'Your father loves you, you know that, don't you?' he murmured, still not taking her lips although she strained up to him, her eyes liquid.

'I know.' As she pulled his head down there was a brilliant heat in his eyes and then his lips met hers, his breath escaping in a deep groan of need. His arms tightened as he felt her response and then he was raining burning kisses over her face, her throat, her closed eyelids, his breathing harsh and ragged and his body taut and hard.

'Katie—' he raised his head, pushing her away slightly as he fought for control '—I can't—I've waited so long. You don't understand what you do to me. If we don't stop now I shall take you, and your chance for dinner will be gone.'

It was a poor attempt to lighten the situation but she had felt the trembling in his body, sensed the desperate waiting in him, and her love for him filled her with a crazy kind of exhilaration that she could affect him so badly. But his desire wasn't love. The thought didn't have the power to stop her lifting up her arms towards him. Her love would have to be enough for them both.

'Katie…' He breathed her name with a soft groan. 'Don't say I didn't warn you; I want to eat you alive…' She smiled, a wild excitement at the knowledge of her power over this hard, fierce man giving her face a primitive sensuality that made his breath catch in his throat.

'I was going to wine and dine you, coax you—'

'Well, coax me, then.' Her voice snapped the last shred of his control and he pulled her into him desperately, moulding her against the length of him, his arousal hot and fierce as his hands explored the length of her. She was hardly aware of her dress sliding to the floor but when her bra followed and he knelt before her, his mouth erotic on her full, taut breasts, she moaned softly, her fingers entwining in the short, crisp black hair of his head as she trembled and shook.

'I told you how it would be between us...' As he rose, lifting her into his arms and carrying her across to the massive bed, she felt a moment's sadness at his whispered words. Yes, he had told her. Told her that their bodies would be good together, that they would be... What had he said? Oh, yes, 'compatible'.

What would he say if she told him it was her love that made her flower at his touch, her love that had evoked a raging thirst for them to become as one? But he must never know. That humiliation, more than any other, would be too much to bear.

He undressed quickly, his eyes never leaving hers as he drank his fill of her, lying pale and trembling in the dusk-filled room, and then he was beside her. His hands removed the last barrier between them, sliding her pants down her legs slowly as he kissed their path with warm, searching lips, and she was unable to stop the shivers of desire shaking her limbs. His body was strong and hard as he took her in his arms again, the feel of his nakedness strange and thrilling even as its alien ability frightened her. She wasn't ready for this... His maleness was too fierce, too powerful...

'Relax, my sweet darling, relax...' He had sensed the

sudden surge of fear at the unknown and his voice was soft and tender against her mouth. 'We have all the time in the world.'

And slowly, surely, he fed her desire with lips that blazed fire over every part of her body as she lay helpless and warm in his embraces, his mouth and hands hungry and sensual, cajoling an aching pleasure that was almost pain until she found herself arching and pleading for a release from the sweet, subtle torment. His lips were demanding as they found and explored all her secret places, the fire that was consuming her burning away any shred of shyness or fear.

And as his hands lifted her hips to meet his body he still continued to ravage her mouth, catching the gasp of fleeting pain as he possessed her fully and kissing away the brief moment of panic with deep, tender kisses until she began to move in rhythm with his maleness, a shuddering ecstasy rippling over her being in greater and greater intensity until it seemed as though she was on fire.

'You are mine, fully mine,' he groaned harshly as he took her with him to the heights that were filled with blinding colour and light, the world exploding into a million glittering pieces that were piercing and hot against her closed eyes.

'Have I hurt you?' His voice was thick and warm with a rueful tenderness as she stirred beneath him, her senses slowly returning as he moved off her and drew her into his side. 'I had promised myself that I would be patient, restrained, that tonight I would let you sleep so that you would be ready to accept my advances tomorrow in the security and warmth of our villa in Spain.'

'Our villa'? Somehow those two words meant more than the physical act of possession in all its intimacy. She was his wife. He had told her that she would be his wife in the full sense of the word, that their lives would be intrinsically linked from this point, and she believed him; she did.

And with such closeness, such familiarity, surely that other love would cease to keep its hold on his mind and his heart? He had promised her that there would be no other women and she knew he believed that was enough but she wanted more than a commitment of bodily faithfulness—she wanted his heart too.

'Katie?' He rose slightly on one elbow to look into her flushed face and she knew in that instant that she must be patient. He wanted her physically; he had shown her tonight that he was capable of tenderness and understanding even in his overwhelming need of her body. From that she would have to cultivate the first seeds of love.

'Yes, you hurt me.' She slanted her eyes at him in mock-severity even as she wanted to reach up and pull his face to hers, to kiss his mouth without passion getting in the way, to trace each line and contour of his hard face with her lips. 'But I forgive you.'

'You do?' He smiled down at her, his eyes lazy as they stroked over her naked body. 'Well, that's a good omen for the future, wouldn't you say?' There was some inflexion, just a shred of emotion she couldn't quite place, in his voice, but she could read nothing from his face and decided she must have imagined it.

'Maybe.' She smiled up at him as he brushed a tendril of hair from her cheek with one finger. She must keep this relaxed and easy; she was feeling too vulnerable for any deep talking, too exposed and close to tears.

'No, not "maybe".' His eyes darkened as he let his finger trail down the length of her body. 'You are mine now, completely and utterly. You belong to me. You made it clear last night that you don't want to talk about how I feel but surely you can see that we need to discuss things? Our future is bound up together, Katie, you can't deny that, and after what we just shared—'

'Please.' She shook her head as she went to move from his side and in the same instant he pulled her back against him, his face suddenly still as his eyes travelled over her troubled face.

'No, don't turn away from me,' he said huskily.

'Can we just take things a day at a time?' she asked weakly as his power over her swamped her afresh. She couldn't, she just couldn't listen to any explanations about Maisie now; even if he didn't put a name to his love she would know whom he was talking about.

He had made it clear at the start why he was marrying her. In that she had no reason to complain. He had laid it fair and square on the line and she had walked into this with her eyes open but... But it hurt like hell.

She didn't want to listen to a reiteration of his promise of physical faithfulness, not now, not when the need for reassurance was so strong that she could taste it. He was a possessive, ruthless and hard man. What he had he kept and he didn't share. She knew that. And as his wife, the vehicle by which his future heir would be born, she was of more value than anything else he possessed.

'Go to sleep, Katie.' His voice was quiet and flat but his arms were gentle as he drew her into him, stroking her hair softly as they lay together in the gathering darkness until the warmth of his body and the steady beat of his heart under her cheek sent her into a deep, dreamless sleep.

She had never seen anything more beautiful than the area of Northern Spain where Carlton's villa was situated.

They left the hotel early the next morning after a huge breakfast and she found herself painfully tongue-tied in the cold light of day when she remembered the intimacies of the night before, although Carlton chatted with an ease that gradually relaxed her taut muscles and freed her tongue.

The plane flight was uneventful and when they landed at the Spanish airport the usual formalities were dealt with quickly and efficiently. As they left the terminal, stepping into the brilliant heat beyond the air-conditioned building, Carlton guided her over to a powerful, low-slung sports car parked in a reserved spot just outside the massive doors.

'Is this yours?' she asked in surprise as he extracted a key from his pocket and opened the back of the car, slinging their cases into the area beyond.

'Uh-huh.' He moved round to open her door, his eyes narrowed against the piercing quality of the light. 'I keep it garaged in the town here and have it brought to the airport when I arrive.'

'Oh, right.' The power of money, she thought to herself as she slid into the luxurious seat and watched him walk round to the driver's side. His wealth seemed to open magic doors, smooth all the normal little irritating difficulties of life clean away. 'That's very convenient,' she added as he slid into the seat beside her and started the engine, which responded immediately.

'Yes, it is.' He extracted two pairs of sunglasses from the front of the car and handed one to her with a smile, the lazy warmth of which took her breath away. As he slipped his own pair on, and his eyes were masked from her gaze, she thought again of the things his mouth and hands had done to her the night before and found her cheeks were burning as she remembered the majestic power of the big male body sitting next to her. She felt vulnerable, helpless, but also more feminine than she had ever done in her life, as well as wonderfully, vitally alive.

They travelled through the town nearest to the airport, and out on a long, winding road the other side, and Katie was spellbound by the intensity of colour in all that she saw: villages of golden stone perched amid pine-clad hills, tall towers of brown churches in the distance with great bells outlined against the startling blue sky, fields of almond, olive, lemon and orange trees shimmering gently in the midday sun and glimpses of picturesque fishing harbours and fine golden beaches set in secluded bays on either side of rocky headlands.

They passed small whitewashed houses set among orange and lemon groves with flowered, walled gardens adjoining the orchards, and several villages where the houses had balconies of wood or iron covered in scarlet geraniums, pink begonias and trailing purple and red bougainvillaea which were a blaze of colour against the whitewashed walls.

'Magnificent, isn't it?' Carlton had been aware of her breathless appreciation of the dramatic scenery and now his voice held a note of indulgent, amused pleasure as she turned to face him, her face flushed and her eyes sparkling behind their protection of dark glass.

'It's just wonderful.' Her eyes studied the dark, impassive profile. 'How long have you had a villa here?'

'My parents bought it before I was born,' he answered quietly. 'My maternal grandmother was Spanish and although my mother was born in England the family were always visiting their relatives over here. Most of them are scattered about the world now—Canada, England, France—but there are a few who still prefer the Spanish sun to any other.'

'I can see why,' she breathed softly as the car began to climb into the mountains. They had just passed a small village, where Katie had been enchanted to see an old brown donkey with a small barefoot child on its back in a square packed with market stalls overflowing with produce, when Carlton drove the powerful car through an open gateway set in a high, ancient wall and into a large garden bursting with trees and shrubs, before drawing to a halt in front of a shadow-blotched, rambling, hacienda-style villa.

'La Casa.' Carlton turned to her as he cut the engine and kissed her very thoroughly before leaving the car to open her door.

'La Casa?' She emerged pink and ruffled to stand beside him, conscious as ever of his great height and the restrained power in his lithe, impressive body.

'Home.' He smiled down at her, suddenly very foreign in the shimmering sunlight, his black hair and smoky grey eyes with their thick black lashes sending shivers down to her toes. 'My mother might have been English but in here—' he tapped his chest gently '—she was always Spanish. She loved it here. Every holiday I had from school, whatever time of the year, we would fly out to La Casa even if it was just for a few days.

'My father rarely came—the businesses took up most of his time and attention—but we would content ourselves nevertheless. At first it was just the two of us but when Joe was born he loved it too.

'I brought him out here after the accident once he was well enough to travel and it turned out to be wonderful therapy. He had been holding on to the past too hard. The last memory he had of my mother and father was their bodies after the crash, before he was cut free, and it was impeding his recovery. It took a few months but eventually La Casa helped him to remember them with more peace than pain.'

'La Casa and you,' she said softly, watching the play of emotions across the hard face. 'It was a terrible time for you too, wasn't it?'

He shrugged, turning away immediately, but she had seen the flash of raw pain in his face before he could speak. 'I survived.' His voice was dismissive, abrupt, but even as she shrank from the rebuff he turned back and touched her face with his hand. 'I'm sorry, Katie; I didn't mean...' He shook his head slowly as he held her hazel eyes with his own. 'I don't find it easy to express my emotions; I never have.'

'You trust very few people,' she whispered softly, repeating the words that he had stated at their first meeting and which had stayed in her mind ever since. And it would appear that she wasn't one of them yet.

'You can't have it all ways.' He stared at her, his eyes very dark in the white light. 'You've made it clear what you want, or don't want, from me, and I'm doing my damnedest to play by the rules, but I can only be pushed so far, Katie. Even this block of stone has his limits.'

'I don't understand.' Her eyes were wide with hurt as she gazed into his face. What had she done now?

'No matter.' He shrugged and smiled and suddenly he was the Carlton of the night before and that morning, relaxed, easy, with a lazy charm that was fascinating. But that wasn't how he was really feeling. As she held his eyes one more moment before he moved to take her hand and lead her into the villa she knew her sixth sense was right. He was playing a part, but why?

The villa was quite breathtakingly lovely inside, with an old, rustic feel to it that hadn't been spoilt by the fine furnishings and modern amenities which Carlton explained had been added at a later date. Most of the whitewashed walls were covered in an array of fine plates, decorated with coloured animals and flowers and glazed thickly like Arab pottery, as well as a host of exquisite pictures.

The front door led directly into the massive sitting-room, which was a blaze of colour in red and gold and stretched the length of the house. The leaded French windows at the far end of the room led out on to a large patio surrounded by orange and lemon trees and gently waving palms. There was also a very large and well-stocked kitchen, with fine oak cupboards and a red tiled floor, a breakfast-room, a more formal dining-room and a downstairs cloakroom complete with a large double shower.

Upstairs, the five bedrooms seemed to stretch for miles, three with their own *en-suite* bathrooms, and all with large balconies covered in red and white bougainvillaea, deep green ivy and the fragile, lemon-scented verbena. The master bedroom and one other overlooked the grounds at the back of the house where an olympic-size swimming-pool, just beyond the fringe of trees surrounding the patio, shimmered gently in the blazing sunshine.

'I can't believe it.' As she stood with Carlton on the balcony of the master bedroom she felt as though she had been transported into another world. All this would have been so perfect, so utterly enchanting if the tall, dark man standing silently by her side had been truly hers with his heart as well as his body. At this moment she would have given every last penny of the Carlton fortune to live with him in a little shack if he had spoken one word of love. 'It's just so lovely.'

'We have two girls in the village who come and air the house periodically and do a little housework,' Carlton said quietly as he stood at her side, his profile dark and austere as his eyes gazed straight ahead. 'If the family are in residence they come each afternoon to prepare and serve an evening meal and attend to the household chores. I've never wanted anyone living in but I can hire a housekeeper on a permanent basis if you would prefer that.'

'No.' As the image of Maisie flashed before her mind she spoke quickly and instinctively. One housekeeper was more than enough.

Katie was always to remember the next few days with a bittersweet enchantment that even in the years ahead could bring tears to her eyes with their painful poignancy. They spent the mornings lazily by the pool, alternately swimming in the cool, silky water and dozing on the luxuriously up-holstered sun-loungers scattered round the tiled edge. After a cold lunch they would set out to explore the surrounding countryside, Carlton's face often relaxed and animated in a way it had never been in England as he showed her the country he loved.

They travelled through mountain villages where patient donkeys still carried the occupants along cobbled, flower-decked streets and twisting, narrow lanes, wandered in green meadows beside peach and cherry orchards set against a mountainous backdrop of jagged limestone, bathed in golden bays of warm, crystalline water and re-turned home each evening, as the soft, gentle dusk began to mellow the fierce sun, to a delicious meal served by the two giggling, dark-eyed girls from the village.

But it was the nights that were the most bittersweet of all, timeless and enchanting as Carlton gradually introduced her to a potent, bewitching world she had only guessed at. As the hours unfolded in all their intimacy she realised that during that first night he had been wonderfully patient and controlled, his passion curbed in view of her innocence, and the knowledge made her love him all the more.

In fact, each day she loved him more as she discovered the man behind the mask. And still there were no words of love in all the passion and desire; still the days and even the nights were marred by moments of electric tension, strain and unease.

It was after one such moment early in the morning, when she had woken to find him leaning on one elbow watching her face in such a way that she had immediately imagined that he was wondering how it would be if his love were there beside him, and had reacted accordingly with veiled eyes and an almost visible withdrawal of her body, that the telephone call came.

She had already gone downstairs and Carlton was in the bathroom, shaving, and so she took the call, wondering nervously if a flood of incomprehensible Spanish was going to meet her ears. 'Hello? This is Katie Reef.' The name was still strange on her tongue. 'Can I help you?'

'Katie?' Joseph's voice was strained and tight. 'I have to talk to Carlton; is he there?'

'Yes, of course, I'll just get him.' She put the receiver to one side and ran quickly up the open, winding stairs that led to the first floor of the villa, her heart thudding as her senses recognised the note of distress and panic in Joseph's voice. What now?

Carlton turned as she entered the bathroom and, as always, her heart went haywire at the sight of him. He was stripped to the waist with just a pair of jeans covering his lower half, and his muscled chest with its light covering of dark body-hair was bronzed and powerful in the light-coloured bathroom. 'Was that the phone I heard?'

'It's Joe,' she said breathlessly as her eyes drank him in.

'Joe?' His eyes narrowed as he shook his head. 'You don't mean to say he's calling us on the first week of—'

'There's some sort of trouble, I think,' she said quickly. 'He seemed upset, Carlton.' Even as she spoke he reached for a towel and wiped the shaving-foam from his face, pushing past her and running down the stairs, Katie following at his heels.

'Joe?' His voice was anxious. 'What's wrong?' He listened for a few moments in silence and then barked a particularly explicit oath down the phone that made Katie jump. 'Why the hell did you let her?' he growled angrily. 'What's the matter with you, anyway?' There followed a few more terse sentences that Katie couldn't make head or tail of, although she gleaned enough to realise that Carlton was furiously angry with his brother, and as he banged the phone down and turned towards her she saw that his face was black with rage.

'The young fool. The stupid, blind young fool,' he muttered grimly. 'If anything's happened to her—'

'What *has* happened?' she asked softly as a terrible sense of foreboding rose like a thick cloud over the magic of the last few days.

'It's Maisie.' As his eyes focused on her face she saw the deep concern and her heart began to pound like an express train. 'She's left the house, disappeared in the middle of the night.'

'In the middle of the night?' She had heard the expression of blood turning to ice but it was the first time she had experienced it.

'She could be anywhere considering the state Joe says she was in.' He ran a hand distractedly through his hair. 'There was no need for this, no need at all. What on earth was Joe thinking of?'

'You can't blame this on Joe!' She was suddenly furiously, fiercely angry, her rage so intense that it swept away every other emotion in its path. So the lovely brunette *was* his mistress and she hadn't been able to stand by and see him married to another woman. She felt sick with impotent fury. What was he doing, playing with all their lives like this? Just who did he think he was?

'You don't understand.' His voice was preoccupied, absent, and the final humiliation was that he was looking through her as though she weren't there. 'Joe—'

'Oh, yes, I do,' she said tightly. 'I'm not a fool, Carlton, and I understand far more than you think. I do have a pair of eyes in my head, you know.' Her blood was pounding in her ears but her eyes were as dry as dust.

'You know?' he asked as he seemed to force himself to concentrate on her. 'Did Joe tell you?'

'No.' She didn't know where this strength that kept her

upright was coming from but she was more than thankful for it. 'I just put two and two together—'

'Joe was supposed to put things right,' Carlton muttered as he walked past her as though he hadn't heard her. 'She must have been in a damn awful state to clear out like that. Hell, he promised me—'

'*He promised you*?' She was shrieking now, all control gone as the absolute unfairness of it all made her quite literally see red. He had left Joseph to do his dirty work, placate his mistress while he played his games thousands of miles away, and now, it having gone all wrong, he was laying the blame on the younger man's shoulders? 'I don't believe I'm hearing this.'

'You don't believe you're hearing what?' The pitch of her voice had got through to him and he turned with his foot on the first step of the stairs and glanced across at her. 'What the hell is the matter with you anyway?'

'What do you think is the matter with me?' she asked furiously.

'I don't know, Katie; that's why I'm asking you.' If she had been rational she would have noticed that he had gone curiously still, his dark eyes intent on her face and his voice low and controlled, but she was too mad to observe the subtle body language and the sudden awareness in the smoky grey eyes that narrowed with disbelief at his own suspicions.

'You expect me to just stand by and say nothing,' she asked incredulously, 'while you panic about where your mistress has gone?'

'My *what*?' And then she realised, as she stared into his face which had gone as white as a sheet, his eyes glittering with a fury that surpassed her own, that she had made a terrible, unforgivable mistake.

CHAPTER NINE

'YOU think Maisie is my mistress?' Carlton asked with a deadly quietness that was more lethal than any roar of rage. 'You've been thinking that all along?'

'I...' Katie's voice faltered and died at the look on his face. 'It seemed like that; I—' She shook her head as she searched for words. 'You were always so nice to her... You—' Her words strangled in her throat. 'You were kind, gentle...'

'And because those attributes are so alien in me, so unnatural, the only conclusion that you could draw was that if I was nice to anyone I was sleeping with her?' he asked softly. 'I'm such an animal in your eyes, so abnormal that I can't feel friendship or warmth or any of the normal human emotions that the rest of the human race takes for granted?'

He hadn't moved any nearer, made any threatening gesture, but she was rooted to the spot with an overwhelming fear of what he might do if she moved so much as an inch. 'You thought I would marry you, commit myself to you when I was using another woman in that way, forcing her to watch us together and even expect her to keep my house?'

She stared at him, her eyes enormous in the chalk-white of her face, as his lips drew back from his teeth in a contemptuous snarl that paralysed her with fright. 'And my fumbling attempts to make you understand how much I loved you—you thought they were all part of the act?' he asked acidly. 'No wonder you cut me dead each time I tried to make you understand how I felt.'

His eyes narrowed still more into black slits that gave

his face a sinister, panther-like darkness. 'And you were prepared to marry me, thinking all that? Sell yourself to such a man as that? What are you, Katie? Who are you? Did your flesh creep each time I touched you? Was all that passion, all that desire an act to keep the buyer happy?'

'Carlton, it wasn't like that.' She was frightened, desperately, helplessly frightened, her mind still reeling from the revelation that he loved her—he loved *her*—but that she had ruined it all, destroyed anything they might have had because he would never forgive her for this. His eyes told her so.

'The hell it wasn't.' His face was grey now, his mouth a hard white slit in a face that was as cold as ice. 'I thought I could *make* you love me, Katie.'

He gave a harsh bark of a laugh. 'Funny, isn't it? The ultimate irony. I couldn't believe that, feeling as I did, you wouldn't respond. Oh, I know you hated me at the beginning, that circumstances conspired to make it all wrong, but the physical chemistry was real—or I thought it was.

'You hit me like a ton of bricks that day you came to the office, when I sat with you on my lap and you sobbed out all your insecurities and pain. But we'd got off to a bad start so I thought I'd play the waiting game, persevere, be around.

'But every time we met there were fireworks and then the solution was dropped in my lap. I could help your father, keep you near me at the same time and show you the man I really was. I was going to be patient, believe it or not.' His face was caustic with self-contempt. 'I wasn't going to force my unwelcome attentions on you, I was going to wait until you were ready, however long it took, because once you had married me I had all the time in the world. No one else could touch you. But then...'

He shook his head slowly. 'What the hell was that on our wedding night, Katie? You didn't have to give satisfaction for money like some whore in a brothel.'

She deserved it. She knew she deserved it but his words

were more punishment that she could bear. The bitter hurt
and pain that had turned his face into a stone mask cut her
like a knife. What had she done? *What had she done*? She
had seen so many glimpses of his caring side even before
they were married and the tenderness he had displayed
since they had been man and wife had touched her time
and time again. She should have known he wasn't capable
of this thing—she should have known, especially loving
him as she did.

'Please, Carlton,' she whispered brokenly. 'Let me explain.'

'You've had your revenge, Katie.' As she went to walk
towards him he lifted his hand to stop her. 'You've shown
me what an arrogant fool I am, but just at this moment the
urge to wring that beautiful neck of yours is overpowering
so just keep your distance for an hour or so,' he warned
with chilling grimness.

'But I want to talk to you,' she pleaded desperately. 'This
isn't what you think—'

'I don't want to talk to you,' he said bitterly. 'In fact I
don't want to look at you, think about you—' He turned
and strode past her, walking to the French doors at the end
of the room and opening them savagely before striding out
on to the patio and disappearing behind the trees.

'*Carlton!*' She screamed his name but there was no reply, just the bright, sun-filled room and warm, scented air
that was a mockery in itself when she could hardly breathe
for the agony that was tearing her apart.

How long she stood there in the screaming silence she
didn't know, but eventually she walked slowly across the
room and up the stairs, entering their bedroom and walking
out on to the balcony that was already hot underfoot with
the heat of the sun. She looked up into the clear blue sky
first, her eyes narrowed against the piercing light, and then
down into the garden below, gazing blindly into space as
her mind whirled and spun.

He had said he loved her. The thought was drumming

loudly in her head along with the sickening, weak feeling in her stomach which the sudden confrontation had produced. Why hadn't he told her before? Then none of this would have happened.

Her mind searched its memories, like a computer compiling data, and suddenly several little incidents, when he had tried to do just that, were stark and clear in front of her. But she had been too blind, too stubborn to deviate from the verdict her brain had decided to reach and now she had lost him.

She whimpered out loud as she gripped her arms round her waist and swung back and forth in an agony of grief, the locket that he had given her on their wedding night moving gently against her throat.

A sudden movement below focused her eyes on the swimming-pool and she saw Carlton's powerful body cutting through the water like a machine, his arms and legs keeping up an unbelievable speed as he swam relentlessly up and down it.

He was nearly an hour in the water and her eyes didn't leave him for a moment, and when at last he hauled himself out to stand naked and magnificent for a moment in the blazing hot sun she saw that his shoulders were bowed as though with an unbearable weight, and the pain was so intense in her throat that she thrust her fist into her mouth to stop herself crying out. She had hurt him, hurt him as no one else had ever done. The knowledge was crucifying.

She watched him as he pulled his jeans on slowly, running a hand through his wet hair as he straightened, and then the big, lean body stiffened, his shoulders squaring and tensing, and she knew he had come to a decision of some kind.

'Pack your things, Katie.' As he joined her in the bedroom she turned to face him, her heart pounding. 'I'll check the first flight to England.'

'We're going back?' There was a lump in her throat that was making speech almost impossible.

'I hardly think there's any point in continuing this travesty, do you?' he asked grimly as his eyes flickered briefly over her tear-stained face before he turned to leave the room. 'Besides which I want to make sure Maisie doesn't do something silly—something Joe might have to live with for the rest of his life.'

'Carlton—'

'Don't offer any platitudes, Katie.' He swung round so savagely that she took an instinctive step backward, her hand going to her mouth as she realised that his veneer of self-control was paper-thin. 'I don't want to listen to a word you might say. Just keep quiet and pack your things.'

They left that day on an evening flight, the tall, dark, stony-faced man and pale, fair-haired slip of an English girl, and no one looking at their faces would have guessed that they were on their honeymoon.

Katie was in the grip of a fear so overwhelming that she was functioning purely on automatic, the guilt and horror of what her hasty words had produced in Carlton almost unbearable. He had retreated behind that invincible authority and coldness that had so misled her in the early days, unassailable and proud and quite unreachable.

All she could hope for was that there would be an opportunity, just a slight mellowing of that icy calm, for her to tell him the truth and bare her soul. But somehow, looking at his face and remembering all he had told her of his past life, she feared he wouldn't let her in even for a moment.

She had tried to talk to him once more before they had left the villa, but at her first words he had cut her off with such bitter ferocity that she hadn't dared try again. He was a fiercely proud man—that much she had known—but now she realised that in acting as she had she had ground that pride into the dust and he was finished with her. It was in his every action, every gesture, every icy glare.

Joseph was at the house when they arrived late that night and the sight of his face, strained and white, reached through Katie's grief and made her want to take that much younger Reef into her arms and soothe his distress like a mother with an unhappy child.

'What happened?' It was clear that Carlton had no such feeling as he put their suitcases down in the hall and spoke directly to his brother who had just wheeled his chair from the sitting-room. 'And I want it all, mind, straight down the line.'

'I didn't expect you to come back.' Joseph glanced from one to the other, his eyes red-rimmed and exhausted. 'Carlton, this is all my fault; you can't say anything to me I haven't already said to myself,' he groaned desperately.

'I wouldn't bank on it,' Carlton said grimly, but his face had softened somewhat at the younger man's obvious desolation. 'I thought you were going to go for it at long last— forget all these damn stupid ideas about being half a man and unable to give her children and so on? You know she's loved you since the moment she put a foot in the house, dammit. What more of a guarantee could you want for a marriage? You've held her at arm's length, made her as miserable as hell ever since I can remember and still she hasn't looked at another man. If that isn't love I don't know what is.'

'I know, I know.' Joe raked his hair desperately, his eyes bleak.

Katie stared at their faces in stupefaction. Maisie and Joe? *Maisie and Joe*? They had loved each other for years but Joe had refused to admit it to her, she thought helplessly as all the little incidents from the past slotted neatly into place. It was clear that Carlton thought they would be the ideal match and all his gentle concern for Maisie, his encouragement to the painfully shy beauty and, she saw now, fatherly affection had been to compensate for Joe's discouragement and rejection. What a mess. She gazed at the two men flatly. What a terrible, hopeless mess.

'Don't say "I know",' Carlton bit out angrily. 'We had this conversation a couple of days before the wedding and you assured me that once you and Maisie were here alone you would set things straight with her and put both of you out of your misery. Hell, I hinted as much to her at the reception just before we left, when she looked so damn miserable. Don't you realise what that day must have been like for her, feeling the way she does about you?'

'I told her we needed a year apart,' Joe admitted bleakly, his broad shoulders pathetically slumped. 'I *was* going to propose to her, Carlton. I even organised a meal with wine, roses, the lot, but then I looked at her across the table and she was so damn beautiful. I couldn't face tying her to a cripple for the rest of her life.'

'So in effect you sent her away?' Carlton asked caustically.

'She asked me why the year apart and I told her she ought to meet someone else,' Joe said flatly. 'Someone who could love her like a real man.'

Carlton ground out an oath as he shook his head in disbelief. 'Dammit, man, you *can* love her like a real man,' he said more softly now. 'The accident only interfered with your procreative ability; everything else down there is in prime working order.'

They seemed to have completely forgotten about Katie, for which she was supremely thankful as the more intimate aspects were discussed.

'You can adopt, can't you? Private adoption, anything. We aren't exactly short of a penny or two in case it's slipped your mind, Joe. Maisie has faced and accepted that she won't have children of her own, you know that. All she wants is you.'

'What am I going to do?' Joseph stared up at his brother helplessly. 'The last twenty-four hours have made me realise I can't live without her, Carlton. What the hell am I going to do?'

'Pray that I find her,' Carlton said grimly. 'Did she take all her things?'

'Everything personal.' Joseph's voice broke and Carlton bent to hug him swiftly, his own face working for a second before he stood up, his eyes thoughtful.

'There's one place she might be—that friend of hers from the children's home that she's kept in touch with through the years,' he said quickly. 'Have you spoken to her?'

'I tried her number,' Joseph said bleakly. 'She said she hadn't seen her.'

'She's a friend, Joe; she would,' Carlton answered drily. 'I'll go round there myself. If she isn't there it'll be down to private detectives—the police won't want to know—but we'll find her, however long it takes.' He patted his brother's shoulder. 'And when we do just keep your mouth shut and take her in your arms, boy, OK? She had one hell of a life in that children's home from when she was a baby; the only thing she wants from you is love.'

His compassion, his understanding rent Katie's heart into ribbons as she stood in the shadows to one side of the hall, watching them. And he had loved her. The only trouble was that she had the sick feeling that the past tense was right. Had.

She sat and listened to Joseph talk through the next few hours in between making them endless cups of coffee and forcing him to eat some sandwiches she prepared. She didn't mention the situation between Carlton and herself; it wouldn't have done any good, and the younger man looked on the verge of collapse as it was.

Dawn was just breaking and Joseph had fallen into a light doze by her side when she heard Carlton's car pull up outside. She rose quickly, careful not to brush against the wheelchair and wake him, and walked out into the hall just as Carlton opened the front door and stood aside to let Maisie walk in.

The lovely brunette looked shattered, drained, and without even thinking about it Katie walked across and hugged her tight, and after a moment of startled surprise Maisie hugged her back. 'He's in there,' Katie said quietly as she gestured towards the sitting-room. 'He's been asleep for a few minutes.'

'I won't wake him.' Maisie looked at her with eyes that were swollen with crying. 'I'll just stretch out on the sofa in there and then I can be around when he wakes up.' She smiled at them both before walking into the room and shutting the door softly after her.

'You found her, then,' Katie said nervously even as she thought what an inane remark it was.

'Yes.' He stood looking at her through shuttered eyes and Katie thought he had never looked more attractive, or more unapproachable. 'She was with her friend. It took me a while to persuade the girl to let me in, but once she realised I wasn't going to go she obliged. She's not too thrilled with the Reef name; I can't blame her.' He shook his head slowly. 'But she is a good friend to Maisie and good friends don't happen too often in a lifetime.'

'No...' She felt glued to the spot and then forced herself to speak quickly before she lost her nerve. 'Carlton, about us—'

'Leave it, Katie.' The armour was back in place instantly. 'I'm damn tired and I don't want any post-mortems right at this moment. I'll move into one of the other bedrooms and I suggest you get a few hours' sleep yourself; you look done in.'

'But I don't want you to move into one of the other bedrooms,' she said rapidly. 'I—'

'I don't care what you want, Katie,' he said flatly, his eyes cold and remote. 'Later on we can discuss how best to handle this—whether you want a divorce straight away or a separation for a time to give your father time to reconcile himself to the situation—but right now I'm going to bed—alone. OK?'

'A divorce?' Somehow, in spite of all that had happened, she hadn't been expecting this and his words hit her like a physical blow. She put a hand to her mouth in protest.

'Don't worry, the financial side will remain as I promised,' he said coldly, misunderstanding her gasp of shock and white face. 'Whatever else I am I don't welsh on a deal. All your father's debts will be cleared and I'll continue to support his business with a nice healthy bank balance to keep him thinking he's winning. Your settlement we can discuss separately, but you won't have to work again or do anything else you don't want to for the rest of your life.'

'I don't want a divorce,' she said numbly.

'A separation, then.' He was already turning and walking up the stairs as he spoke. 'You can play this exactly how you want to. You kept your end of the bargain after all— you married me and fulfilled all your marital duties.' His voice was derisive and tight but even through the cynicism her new awareness of him heard the agonised pain he was trying to hide.

'You won't listen to me, then?' she asked quietly, moving to stand at the bottom of the stairs. 'Hear how sorry I am?'

'I accept your apology, Katie.' His eyes were narrowed and veiled as he looked down at her from the first floor. 'And I absolve you of all guilt, all blame; how about that? You are free to leave if that's what you want or stay until the legal formalities are completed. I probably got exactly what I deserved after all in forcing you into a situation I knew you didn't want. But it's over now.' There wasn't a shred of indecision in his voice. 'Finished.'

For one more moment he watched her standing, pale and small, in the hall below, then turned without another word, and as she heard the door to one of the bedrooms close a few seconds later it was as though it was synonymous with all she could expect from the future.

CHAPTER TEN

KATIE remained standing staring upwards in the dimly lit hall for a long time. There was no sound from the sitting-room where Maisie and Joe were or from the bedrooms upstairs. All was quiet and still. She fingered the locket at her neck, her mind too heavy and dull with exhaustion and pain for coherent thought.

She found herself in the sleeping garden almost without being aware of getting there, sinking down on to a wrought-iron bench beneath the sweeping fronds of an old weeping willow tree as her trembling legs finally gave in.

The June morning was just beginning to stir, the birds twittering and calling in the trees surrounding the green square of lawn and a few insects buzzing quietly on their early morning call to the flowering bushes and plants per-fuming the summer air. She sat there as the last of the dawn's shadows were banished by the sun overhead, its mild heat gentle on her arms already browned by the fierce Spanish sun.

'What am I going to do?' She spoke her thoughts out loud, her voice flat and slow. 'I love him. Doesn't that count for anything?' As her gaze wandered round the hushed, tranquil garden she touched the locket again, un-fastening it suddenly and opening it to peer at her mother's face.

'Help me, Mum.' She felt like a little child again, tiny and alone. 'Tell me what to do. I can't let him go; I have to do something.' The tears were raining down her face; it was probably that which gave the minute face a different expression for a moment, but suddenly she heard her

179

mother's voice in her mind as clearly as though she were
in the garden with her.

'Tell him.' The tone was urgent. 'Tell him how you feel.'

'He won't listen,' she answered wearily. 'He's finished
with me; he's had enough.'

'He'll listen.' The voice was persistent. 'He loves you.
Did you have enough of your father over the years? Did
you finish with him because he was wrong, cruel even?
You loved him and love is stronger than disappointment
and bitterness and hurt—yes, and even betrayal. He'll listen. You have to make him listen and then he will understand. He loves you, pumpkin; he'll never love anyone else.
You owe it to him to make him see how you feel, how
wrong you were.'

'Pumpkin'. The old pet name, forgotten through the
years, brought her to her feet. 'Mum?' But there was no
answer, no soft hand on her brow or fleeting shadow that
she could touch, just the silent, peaceful garden and her
own tears.

He was sleeping when she slipped in beside him after
shutting the bedroom door quietly, her heart in her mouth.
The strong, hard face was younger, boyish in sleep; the
harsh lines of experience and life had eased and mellowed.
He stirred very slightly, murmuring her name, before his
breathing regulated and quietened again.

How could she have thought him capable of what she'd
accused him of? she thought as she lay propped on one
elbow, watching him sleep in the same way he had done
with her only the morning before. First Penny and then
Maisie...

She shut her eyes tight as she groaned in her mind. He
had given her so much and she had thrown it all in his face,
and if she had to debase herself now, crawl and plead and
beg, she would. Pride and self-preservation had no place in
her feeling for him any more—they couldn't have.

She had intended to keep awake, fighting the warm blanket of sluggishness every time it descended on her as she

lay curled up by his side, knowing she had to stay awake to confront him the moment he woke, but when something heavy brought her out of a deep inertia she knew by the length of the afternoon shadows that she had slept.

Carlton's arm had landed across her middle and a moment or two later his eyes opened slowly, their lids heavy with sleep. As he saw her by his side he smiled lazily for a split-second and then, as realisation hit, sprang upwards so violently that the bed bounced.

'What are you doing here?' he asked harshly, but she had seen him glance at her naked breasts, seen the hunger in his eyes before he'd swung his legs over the side of the bed, intending to move away.

'Don't go.' She flung her arms round his neck as she pressed herself against his back. 'Please don't go, Carlton, please.'

'Let go of me.' His voice was thick and husky. 'I don't know what you think you're doing but I'm fully aware that this is beyond the call of duty.'

'Carlton, I love you,' she gabbled rapidly, keeping her arms tight round his neck although he had made no move to stand once she had touched him. 'I've loved you for ages but I thought you didn't love me—'

'Katie—' his shoulders tensed, the muscles hard and tight against her soft nakedness, but still she wouldn't let go, hanging on to him as though her life depended on it '—what is this? Some extreme form of guilt? You don't have to lie. I know how you feel and I can handle it. I'm a big boy now—'

'You don't know how I feel,' she said desperately. 'Every time I try to tell you you walk away, and I don't blame you, not after what I thought. But you have to listen.

'I didn't understand before—about you loving me, I mean. I thought you were talking about Maisie, not me. You never made it plain. You never *said*,' she added breathlessly as she tried to fight the sobs that were constricting her throat. 'You'd said at the beginning that you wanted me because I was suitable, that you wanted children, but you never said you cared about me. I know you wanted me physically but then I started to care about you and it wasn't enough. I could see how you were with Maisie—so gentle and protective...'

'Joe was ripping her apart,' he said gruffly without turning his head. 'She was an emotional mess.'

'I now that *now*.' She was frantic. 'But at the time, when you admitted there was someone you loved, it seemed only logical that it was her.'

'Katie, I don't believe you.' He took a deep breath and tried to raise himself but she was a limpet round his neck. 'I've seen the way you look at me, for crying out loud. If all this is through some misguided sense of pity—'

'I won't let you go,' she said brokenly. 'I won't. I love you; I'll always love you even if you hate me. I loved you when we made our marriage vows and they meant exactly what they said to me.' Her arms tightened around him as she covered his neck in desperate, frantic kisses and when he stood he raised her with him, her arms clinging round his neck.

'Let go, Katie,' he said softly. 'This is doing neither of us any good.'

'No, you have to stay with me.' She began to sob even as she fought to stay in control. 'If you leave me, if you make me go there will never be anyone else for me, Carlton. I'll grow old all by myself and I've been by myself so long...' Her voice ended in a wail that wasn't in the least attractive but there was nothing she could do about it.

As he loosened her hands from about his neck, forcing her arms apart as he turned to face her, she couldn't see his face for the tears blinding her eyes. But he was going to go. That thought was uppermost and with it went the last of her fragile control. 'Don't you dare leave me!' she stormed through her sobs. 'Don't you dare. I can't live without you—'

'Shush, my formidable little wife, shush...' And sud-

denly, miraculously, she was held close to his hard, strong
body as he joined her on the bed, pulling her to him as he
kissed the hot, salty tears before taking her mouth in a deep,
long kiss, parting her lips and exploring its full sweetness
with his tongue. 'No more. No more tears.' His hands
cupped her face as he raised himself slightly to look down
into her drowning eyes, his voice husky and not quite even.

His hands moved over her body slowly and sweetly and
he kissed where they lingered, his lips warm and sensual
as they made her nerves quiver and melt with a flood of
tiny, intimate caresses that were delicate and skilfully
erotic.

There wasn't an inch of her body that he left unexplored,
his hands and mouth taking their time as they slowly
brought her to fever pitch, and then the need was raging,
overpowering, taking control of her thoughts and senses
and burning away the agony of the previous twenty-four
hours with its fire. And for the first time endearments and
sweet, intimate phrases of love were spoken as they
touched and tasted and enjoyed.

As molten fire burnt in the moist, warm centre of her
being her body began to tremble and shudder for the release
only he could give, and he moved over her, entering her
fiercely and possessively, murmuring her name against her
lips, and the universe shattered into a million blinding frag-
ments for them both.

When it was over he held her close for a long, long time
without speaking, stroking her hair as she lay entwined with
him, her eyes shut and her mouth content. 'Don't leave
me!' Her voice was urgent and intense when at last he
stirred, her eyes opening wide and shooting to his to read
his expression, displaying her vulnerability for him to read.

'I wouldn't dare.' His lazy smile held both tender amuse-
ment and rueful wistfulness as he kissed her mouth gently.
'I can't remember the last time I was shouted at like that.
You have no respect for your husband, Mrs Reef.'

'Carlton?' She nestled into his shoulder, wrapping her

legs round his as though to anchor him to her side forever. 'You believe me? You aren't going to send me away?'

'I don't think I would have been able to let you go in the final analysis, Katie.' The dark face was very serious. 'It does me no credit but the thought of another man touching you makes me want to commit murder.' She moved to look into his face and saw that he wasn't joking.

'I don't want any man to touch me but you,' she said lovingly, her fingers tracing an idle path across the strong, muscled chest. 'I *do* love you, Carlton. I never want to face another twenty-four hours like the last—'

His mouth descended on hers with a passionate ferocity that stopped further talk, and her desire rose to meet his, her response without inhibition now that she knew she had his heart as well as his body. They soared into a timeless, enchanted world of their own where there was no yesterday or tomorrow, only the present in all its richness. And this time their union had a sweetness, a depth that was like nothing she had ever imagined.

'I wonder if we just made a baby?' She was still enfolded in his arms and now the night sky was dark and strewn with a million tiny, sparkling pinpoints of light, the bedside lamp at the side of Carlton bathing the room in a rosy, subdued glow that gave their naked bodies the texture of silk.

'I hope not.' His words startled her and in spite of the reassurance of the last few hours she raised her head sharply to look into his eyes, relaxing when she saw that they were lit with a soft, tender warmth that melted her bones. 'I'm selfish enough to want you all to myself for a while,' he admitted softly. 'You've married a very possessive man, my love.'

'I know.' She sighed happily. 'Tell me again when you first fell in love with me.'

'Little toad...' He turned her over and slapped her rounded behind before drawing her to him again. 'You put me through hell on earth and then you expect compliments? Just like a woman.'

'Have there been many—women, I mean?' she asked carefully, although his eyes noticed the flash of pain on her quiet face.

'None that has touched my heart.' His dark face was suddenly very still. 'I thought I loved Penny for a time but it only took a little while for me to realise that what I had felt was a blind infatuation, a youthful dream of something that never really was. And then I was searching, without realising it, without ever admitting it to myself—searching for the one woman I could love and want for the rest of my life.'

'Me,' she said with great satisfaction, the last lingering doubts from the past laid finally to rest.

'You.' He raised himself on one elbow and searched her face with his eyes. 'Even your face in that photograph pierced my heart in a way that was both uncomfortable and disturbing and when I met you, breathing hell-fire and damnation, I still told myself that what I felt was a strong sexual attraction—until the minute I took you in my arms, that was. From that moment on I knew I loved you, but it would have been more than my life was worth to try and make you understand how I felt at that time.'

'I wouldn't have believed you,' she admitted ruefully. 'I thought you were like my father, hard and callous, and by the time he explained why he'd been so cold over the years there was Penny and Maisie.'

'And now there is just us.' He kissed her hard. 'And from this moment on we talk about every little thing, every worry, so there can be no misunderstandings between us again.'

'You think you can do that?' she asked in loving disbelief.

'I will try,' he promised gravely. 'And now we should go and see if this stupid brother of mine has finally done the thing I have been urging him to do for years. I'm surrounded by stubborn people in this family.' He eyed her with mock-severity. 'When will you all understand that I know best?'

It was much later, as the four of them sat having a midnight supper in the soft warmth of the June night, that Joseph and Maisie outlined their plans for the future.

'That house I designed for the Croxleys is up for sale,' Joseph said quietly as he sat holding Maisie's hand, their faces relaxed and at peace as though they had just come through a great storm. 'I'd like to put in an offer. With their son being disabled, all the alterations another place would need are already taken care of and they'll be glad of a quick sale now that his new job in America has been finalised. There's a massive downstairs study which would be ideal for my work and the garden is a pocket handkerchief that Maisie will easily cope with.'

'Are you sure you want to leave here?' Carlton asked Joseph softly, although Katie sensed he had been pleased at the proposal.

Joseph had obviously caught the same notion because there was a twinkle in his eye and a wicked tilt to his head as he gazed back at his brother. 'I don't think Maisie and I could stand the noise,' he murmured innocently, with a sidelong glance at Katie that held both respect and admiration. 'I have the strangest feeling you've met your match in Katie, Carlton. I've often longed to shout at you but I've never had the bottle.'

Katie blushed to the roots of her hair but Carlton's face was lazy and unconcerned as he grinned back at the younger version of himself. 'It wouldn't have had the same effect,' he admitted drily.

'We'd like to get married in a few weeks. Neither of us wants any fuss—just a few close friends and family,' Joseph continued quietly, with a long glance at Maisie's lovely face. 'But you'll be my best man?'

'Well, I sure as hell wouldn't let anyone else be,' Carlton

said with a flash of his old arrogance, which made Katie smile and Joseph grin wryly.

'And the Croxleys' house…?'

'That'll be down to you to sort out, Joe, my lad,' Carlton said firmly as he stood up, pulling Katie up with him and wrapping a possessive arm round her waist. 'Just in case anyone has forgotten, this is supposed to be our honeymoon and we're back out on the first plane to Spain tomorrow morning.'

'We are?' Katie queried breathlessly.

'We are.' His eyes were dark and hot as they left the others and mounted the stairs to their room. 'I want to hold you in my arms all night and most of the day without anyone else around, my sweet love. I want to look at you spread out before me in the moonlight and know that you are mine to touch and taste and love. I want to feel your body quiver and tremble beneath mine as I possess every part of you until the only thing you can think of is me.'

As they entered the bedroom he pulled her against him fiercely, his eyes glittering with desire. 'I can't get enough of you, do you know that? You're like a drug, a hypnotising, powerful drug that has enslaved me.'

'Carlton…' Her legs were ready to give way beneath her, so sensual were his words, spoken in that deep, husky voice that made love to her all by itself.

He ran his hands over her skin, satin-soft and honey-brown from the heat of the Spanish sun, as he stripped her swiftly until she stood naked and trembling before him. 'You are my love, my life,' he whispered softly as his eyes blazed over her body. 'My yesterdays, my tomorrows, my wild, sweet destiny…'

And then there was nothing but the blinding, hot darkness of the night as love consumed them both.

Take 2 bestselling love stories FREE
Plus get a FREE surprise gift!

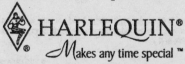

HARLEQUIN PRESENTS®

Anything can happen behind closed doors!
Do you dare to find out...?

Four of your favorite Presents® authors have explored this delicious fantasy in our sizzling new miniseries *Do Not Disturb!*

Fate throws four different couples together in a whirlwind of unexpected attraction. Forced into each other's company whether they like it or not, they're soon in the grip of passion—and definitely *don't* want to be disturbed!

Starting in September 1998 look out for:

September 1998
THE BRIDAL SUITE by Sandra Marton (#1979)

October 1998
HONEYMOON BABY by Susan Napier (#1985)

November 1998
THE BEDROOM INCIDENT by Elizabeth Oldfield (#1994)

December 1998
THE BRIDAL BED by Helen Bianchin (#1996)

Available wherever Harlequin books are sold.

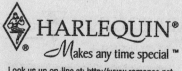

HARLEQUIN®

Makes any time special ™

SEXY, POWERFUL MEN NEED
EXTRAORDINARY WOMEN WHEN THEY'RE

Destined for Love

Take a walk on the wild side this October
when three bestselling authors weave wondrous stories
about heroines who use their extraspecial abilities to
achieve the magic and wonder of love!

HATFIELD AND McCOY
by HEATHER GRAHAM POZZESSERE

LIGHTNING STRIKES
by KATHLEEN KORBEL

MYSTERY LOVER
by ANNETTE BROADRICK

Available October 1998
wherever Harlequin and Silhouette books are sold.

HARLEQUIN®
Makes any time special ™

Silhouette®